KALIFORNIA BLU

Kendell Shaffer

KALIFORNIA BLU

Cover design: Jefferson Eliot
http://www.jasperlark.com
Photo by David Bertolami
http://www.DMBimagery.com
Author Services: Write Spa
http://www.writespa.com
Author website: Tom Stier
http://www.tomstier.com
Visit the author website:
http://www.kendellshaffer.com

ISBN: 978-1-939980-03-8 (ebook)
ISBN: 978-1-939980-02-1 (paperback)

Published by: JasperLark Press

For Sydney Lark and Jasper

ACKNOWLEDGMENTS

Many thanks to Samantha Stier, May Paddock, Maggie Ehrig, Sean Johnson, Alexander Eliot, Atalya Boytner, Anna Shaffer, Tom Stier, Alise Cayen, Matt Gaudio and the Silly Girls. My wonderful editor, Winslow Eliot. Natalya Kaminskaya for posing. David Bertolami for shooting. And to Jefferson Eliot, my partner in crime.

Chapter One

The surf is high tonight, the shore break smashing loud, but down in the bowl I can barely hear it. I'm flat on my stomach, catching my breath. Kinda rough fall, but no real damage. It's dark; no moonlight gets through the low clouds, but they glow from the city lights so there's just enough light to skate by. This is the raddest skateboard park ever, right on Venice Beach, carved into the sand. It's got rails, ramps, steps, linked shallow bowls and one big, deep bowl just like a real empty swimming pool. It makes no sense you can't use it at night. Anyway, it's three o'clock in the morning, what are the chances they'll catch us? They never have before.

I listen to Dakota drop in, swoop around me and grind to a stop. Then his lanky body is leaning over me and sucking on my neck.

"Quit it." I push him away.

I get up, grab my board, and clamber up the side. The ocean's loud up here. I position my board on the lip, ready to drop. It's perfect. Everything is perfect; the pitch-black ocean roaring like monsters, the lights of the city off beyond the boardwalk. Nobody around. Warm breeze. Dakota gets himself out of the bowl and sets up next to me.

"Blazing," he says.

What? The bowl? Me? He takes off his shirt and tucks it inside his jeans. Oh, him. He's lean and strong and his pale skin catches the light. He drops in first, down the side and up the other end on his Civilian board. I'm right behind him squatting down low on my Silly Girl Slayer board and loving the ride. We get into a groove, circling, whirling, swooping round and round. Insane.

"Whoooop."

Dakota jumps off his board. "Leg it, Kal. Po-Po," he yells.

It sounds again: "Whoooop."

We both power up the side, landing on the rim. Sure enough, a police SUV is rolling at us over the sand, its brights bouncing in our faces. Dakota takes off running, heading south, towards the graffiti walls. I head north. There's two cops and they both choose me to chase. But I'm going over the skate park wall, down to the bike path; The SUV can't move around here too easily, especially with all the palm trees. One of the cops jumps out of the SUV and starts chasing me on foot. The SUV blasts sand from under its wheels as it circles round, cuts me off, a female cop leaping out, grabbing my blonde dreadlocks, wrapped with yarn. Oh shit. I squirm away and keep running. I am not letting her take me down. I am not getting arrested.

Never look back. I learned that the semester I was on the swim team: it slows you down.

But I can't hear her behind me anymore. I look back; she's not chasing me. She's on the ground holding her leg. She must have slipped on the sandy concrete. I'm going to get away. So why is she looking at me so smug?

What an idiot I am 'cause I run right into her partner's arms.

Chapter Two

The cop lady is sitting at her desk with a cold Diet Coke can resting on her right knee. The other knee is all bloody below her shorts.

"What'd you go and look back for? You could have gotten away," the cop lady says. I'm sitting in a chair at her desk and she's just moved her chair way too close in front of me.

I look down at my sneakers, green and black checkerboard Vans. I bite my chipped nail polish; it matches: green and black checkerboard too. I ignore her. Cop lady is looking at me like I'm a dead seal or something.

"You're fifteen years old, in the middle of the night, running from cops. What kind of future do you have?"

I hate that. I don't have to talk to her. I know that much.

"Why you squirming? Like a little kid."

I'm not squirming. She's messing with me. She keeps going.

"Don't worry: that's good. It means there's a real person somewhere inside, trying to get out. Am I right?"

I work hard to sit still, sit up, sit tight, staring back, real chill. Then for no reason she laughs at me.

"I was fifteen the first time I was arrested. Doing something stupid like you. I'm not laughing at you, I'm laughing at myself. Nobody in my family believed in me. But I proved them wrong. You got someone in your family you want to prove wrong?"

Oh, yeah, starting with my mom... my mom, who couldn't even bother answering the phone when I called her. Had to leave a message. She better get here soon. I can't take this for much longer.

Cop lady tosses me a brochure from her desk. The cover reads: *TEEN COURT Enabling teens to become responsible citizens.*

"If you decide you want to prove somebody wrong, then Teen Court is the place for you. But remember, you only get one second chance."

I stick the brochure in my back pocket.

Another cop, a big guy with a tight uniform, comes in. "Your attorney is here to pick you up."

"What? What about my mom?"

"What about her?"

I don't want the cop lady to see how irritating it is to have a mom who's too damn lazy to get her butt out of bed and come pick me up herself.

The cop lady gets up and kind of pushes me to follow the other cop into the lobby. She talks in my ear as we cross the room. "I'm doing you a big favor here, but don't misrepresent it in your mind that I like you or anything. My knee hurts like hell, and you're a selfish girl." She steps in front of me, blocking my way, and glares into my eyes. "But I could be wrong," she says slowly. She's still blocking my way.

I can hear Chandara speaking fast and loud in Hindi on her cell phone. Cop lady hears her too and lets me pass into the lobby area. Chandara looks up at me all annoyed, hangs up, and shakes her head like she's my big sister or something. But she's not; she's my mom's lawyer's assistant. She is originally from India but moved here to go to college. She's got this super long hair that goes down past her butt. She wears it in a pony tail and it swishes back and forth when she shakes her head at me.

"Really? Four o'clock in the morning I get a call?"

"My mom call you?"

"No, Bernie called me. From New York. Your mom called Bernie, from the airport."

"Airport? Where's she going?"

"I don't do itineraries. Anyway, Bernie's not thrilled about this. Me neither, by the way. I was at my boyfriend's, in the Valley."

Bernie is her boss, the lawyer. Mom calls her the Big Gun.

I try to lighten things up. "No traffic, at least." It doesn't work. We are not getting along.

Chandara signs for me. The lady cop hands me my cell phone and skateboard.

We go outside; I can't see, it's so bright, the early morning sunlight. The Venice Beach Police Station is a round concrete bunker, about a hundred yards from the skate park. The lack of windows makes it hard to see if anyone's inside. Fooled me last night.

Chandara is busy texting.

"I didn't ask you to handle it. I asked my mom."

"Well, your mom isn't coming, is she? So here I am bailing

12

you out of another mess. And Bernie is gonna try to keep you out of jail and you'll just keep getting into trouble and I'll have to keep dealing with you."

"I never got arrested before. This is the first time and you know it."

"Well, you've just been very lucky."

"Maybe I don't need your help." I'm really tired and the sun is stinging my eyes so I turn and walk away.

"Don't turn your back on me, missy. How are you gonna get home?"

"I'll walk."

"Yeah, right. C'mon. We need to talk strategy. The police are threatening you with some heavy shit and Bernie's gonna want to…"

I can't take it. I run. What's she going to do, chase me in her three inch high heels? I run over the grass hills, out of sight of the cop station, onto the boardwalk. And I don't look back.

At Westminster Avenue I stop. She hasn't followed me. She's probably relieved; probably off to get her nails done or take a yoga class or whatever stuck-up lawyer assistants do when they feel put upon.

The last time I saw Chandara was when my mom forgot me in Joshua Tree. We were in the desert soaking in the hot springs when my mom hooks up with some actor from a TV show. The two of them took off in the middle of the night and left me there. I didn't have a ride back to L.A. At first it was cool. I'm floating around the pool and ordering room service like crazy, but then the hotel manager starts getting some attitude so I call Bernie and she sends Chandara out in heavy weekend traffic to bring me back. I don't think she ever forgave me. The thing is I don't think Chandara hates me, I just think she hates her job. Which includes me.

I walk around the boardwalk for a while. A few vendors are just starting to set up their stalls. A little later this place will be swarming, crawling with people. Now it's so empty, a few homeless types hanging on the grassy bank, a guy carving a life-size mermaid out of wet sand, a fortune teller setting up a small, ornate tent and a teen girl with long stringy hair laying out hippy jewelry on a table. Every day the same. The hand-painted scenes of Venice guy is just arriving, dragging his cart behind his bicycle. Later there will be the incense stall, with bundles of sage, and next to him little glass hand-blown animals. Next to that will be the most useless thing of all: Your Name in Bent Wire. Come to think of it, that's pretty useful compared to another one further up the boardwalk: Your Name on a Grain of Rice.

A block in from the Boardwalk on Westminster is Zelda's, a tiny deli on the corner of Speedway, the narrow alley behind the boardwalk. I order a bag of mini donuts and a carrot, lime and coconut juice. I watch the donuts plop out of the mini donut machine into the oil, then a metal tray flips the donuts completely upside down. They float happily in the bubbly oil until the hot deli guy scoops them out with a spatula and tips them into a brown paper bag.

"Sugar, right?" he asks. He looks about seventeen or eighteen, I guess, with shaggy sun bleached hair.

"Lots." I watch him sprinkle sugar into the brown bag then shake it like crazy.

"They're really hot," he warns as he hands me the bag with

a grin.

I flash him my big grin that says, *so are you*. The grin that inevitably gets me in trouble and could make me cut school and end up spending all day in his VW.

"What's your name?" I ask.

"Van. What's yours?" He smiles one of those cute half grins, like he's trying to be cool, but can't help himself.

"Kalifornia," I tell him. But I'm in enough trouble for one morning, so I'll be good and leave this poor stranger alone to play with his oily dough.

"Kalifornia with a K," I call back as I'm out the door.

I head back to the boardwalk, across the grass, over the bike path and across the wide beach towards the water. The beach is like a little desert, it's so huge. At the shore I settle down in the sand to eat and contemplate what to do next.

My phone rings. It's Dakota. I'm guessing he didn't get caught.

I answer. "'Sup?"

"You get busted?"

"Yeah."

"Are you in jail?"

"No, I'm on the beach. My mom's lawyer's assistant bailed me out."

"You gonna go to school?"

I lie back in the sand. "No, I think I'll just hang out in Venice. Maybe I'll go for a swim."

"All right. I'll call you later. Peace out."

"Later."

I hang up, lay my phone on my stomach and reach into the donut bag. They're still warm. I close one eye and hold a donut up to the sky and look through it. The sugar crystals are glimmering.

A corporate jet from Santa Monica airport flies high over me. I wonder if that's the one my mom is on. Where's she going? I'm guessing her travel assistant sent me an email about her trip. My mom's not worried that I got arrested. She's been arrested so many times. I think she's been waiting for me to get a record. I thought I was smarter than her though. I thought I'd never get arrested.

I pop the donut into my mouth. Then I pull the brochure about Teen Court out of my pocket. It starts all dramatic with: *A Second Chance.*

The plane disappears over the horizon and I wonder when I'll hear from my mom. I pick up my phone. I think about calling her again, but instead I dial the phone number that's printed on the bottom of the Teen Court brochure.

Chapter Three

There's no lawyer here. I'm looking at the customers outside Abbot's Habit coffee shop, but it's the middle of the afternoon on a Wednesday, in Venice. These people don't work. They're mostly half-dressed, slumming with their dogs at tables made of scrap plywood and 2x4s.

Wait, one guy is dressed bad-ass. He looks fine, too: tall with light brown skin. Really short hair and little round glasses. Retro button-down shirt and jeans. He's texting on his cell phone, sipping a latte from a paper cup. But I'm looking for a lawyer, and this guy's a teen. Embarrassing, he caught me staring. Now he's calling me over. Hey, I wasn't staring like *that*... Actually, I was.

I skate up to him and stop. I pop my board and hold onto it. He puts out his hand to shake. So I do. Nice hand. Anyway, he doesn't shake it; more like holds it for a long moment.

"You Kalifornia Blu Cooper?"

"How'd you know?"

"Maybe 'cause I'm here to meet you?"

"Oh. I thought I was meeting a Mr. Roth."

"Yeah."

"You work for him?"

"I am him," he laughs. "I'm a lawyer for Teen Court."

I look at him over my big, green Kate Spade sunglasses. He's checking me out, but trying to hide it. I'm looking pretty good in my Brandy Melville knitted halter-top and slade-fit jeans. My dirty-blonde dreadlocks are down hanging over my shoulders.

"I'm Penn. Penn Roth."

"You mean, Ben? Short for Benjamin?"

"No. Penn, short for Independence."

"What sort of name is Independence?"

"What sort of name is Kalifornia? You want some coffee?"

"Nope."

"You don't like coffee?"

"Nope."

"Well, sit down then and tell me what happened last night. In your own words."

Don't tell me what to do and I need to get one thing clear so I tell him: "I'm not sure I want to do this Teen Court thing."

"Then don't waste my time," he snaps. But I don't mind 'cause I know he's just embarrassed I caught him looking at my belly button ring. I can't blame him, though: it's close and right at his eye level. I give him a bit of a smile.

"How old are you?" I ask.

"I'm sixteen. I've been trained, if that's what..."

I interrupt: "Then you can't be a lawyer." I shouldn't mess with him like this. He's trying so hard not to stare at my belly ring, I almost pity him. But I don't. He sort of sighs. "I'm in a Law School Magnet High School. You're my assignment. I take you through Teen Court and then I get some extra credit which will get me into a decent college and I can get the hell out of this freak show of a town."

"Venice isn't so bad. I like it." I notice this old guy next to me wearing all white with bubble gum pink fingernails so long they start to curl after about four inches.

"If Venice isn't so bad then how come you're out in the middle of the night getting arrested, then turn up in the middle of the day wearing nothing but a bikini top made out of string and with metal all over your body for a meeting with your attorney?" His voice gets really loud at the end.

"If you hate this place so much, how come you didn't wanna meet at Starbucks in the Marina?" Marina Del Rey is the next town over; full of conservative lawyer types like he's turning out to be.

"I like the lattes here. Now let's get on with this." He seems to have no patience for me. I sit down and start to tell him about my arrest. He's pretty serious. He's taking notes like everything I say is important. He rolls up his sleeves. Real strong forearms with long veins sticking out. That gets me every time. Can't go there. This is some stupid-ass lawyer type. I hate lawyers. All of them.

"You want to be a lawyer when you grow up?" I ask.

"Mmmhmmm." He's still writing. The muscles in his forearms flex. I wonder what they feel like? I look all concerned for his future and reach over to hold his arm and inquire:

"Why do you want to do something stupid like that?" Unfortunately this remark makes him take his arm away, but not before it tenses nicely.

"What do you know about lawyers anyway? Your daddy

one?"

"No, my daddy isn't one. I've spent plenty of time with lawyers and let me tell you none of them are decent people."

"Says the criminal."

"Hey."

He puts a piece of paper down on the table and shoves a pen at me.

"Sign here. It says you agree to having your case heard at Teen Court."

What else can I do? I don't want to go to Juvie. I sign. He hands me another sheet of paper.

"Tomorrow at three-thirty sharp, Venice Beach High School. You need to get your parents, at least one of them, to be there. You live with your mom, right?"

"What if she can't come?" My mom is so not coming. I don't even know where she is. Does this mean I have to go to jail if she doesn't show? Shit.

"What about your dad?"

"Haven't seen my dad since I was a little kid."

That seems to stop him cold. "For real?"

"I was eight. It was around my birthday."

"I was six," he says. "My dad didn't come home one day. Never came home."

I don't know what to say. Bummer? I feel your pain? That's a lie: I don't feel anything. Okay, so that's a lie too. What an idiot I am; I never tell anyone about my dad, ever, specifically because I don't want to talk about it. And here I go telling some kid who I don't even know about it. I'll say it's a private matter... that's so B.S. I know: I'll make him talk, so I don't have to. Ask him about his experience... but I don't really want to open up *his* can of worms... maybe he's thinking the same thing because he doesn't seem to want to talk about it any more than I do. He just looks at me, only differently, like he can see a little deeper under my skin. So I change the subject.

"Three-thirty. Got it. I'll be there. With my mom."

He looks me up and down. "And dress up. It's court. Show some respect for the law. Try and wear a skirt. And lose the metal."

"My rings? Are you kidding?" I touch my right earlobe.

But he's walking away.

What a pain in the ass. A skirt? Who is he to tell me what to wear?

I look down at the paper I'm holding and it says if you don't bring a parent to Teen Court then your case is turned back to Juvenile Court. Oh god. That would truly suck.

I take a deep breath and speed dial my mom.

It goes right to voicemail. I don't leave a message. Not another. Not again.

Chapter Four

W hat'd I tell you about dressing? Girl, this is important."
Penn is looking at me like I hurt his feelings. We're
standing outside the auditorium of Venice Beach High School.
It's three-thirty in the afternoon. It's a super-old building with
a big sun-burned front lawn.

I guess a short jean skirt–okay, extremely short skirt–and
suspenders don't count in his book. I was thinking I was
looking tight.

"I'm wearing a skirt. You said, 'try to wear a skirt.'"

"And what about all that metal? I told you to lose the
metal."

"I took out my nipple rings."

Bingo. He blushes underneath that cappuccino skin. He
rolls his eyes, checks his cell, then my breasts. I wasn't lying.
But I'm not taking out my eleven earrings. Not even for him.

"Where's your old lady?

"I don't know."

"You told her three-thirty?"

"Yep."

"You told her South Hall?"

"Lay off. I don't know where she is."

"She knows if she doesn't show, you don't stand a chance?"

"I'll explain to the judge."

"No you won't."

Now he's really pissing me off. "I told her."

The school bell rings.

The hallway turns into a sea of high school students. The big door in front of us swings open, pushed by a kid who is actually dressed in a police uniform. Seriously, this skinny high school student is wearing a cop uniform complete with an LAPD badge over his left pocket.

"Well, hopefully she'll show up soon." Penn leads me into the school auditorium. It still smells like today's lunch. I guess it doubles as the cafeteria. There's a janitor mopping up at the other end of the room.

Penn points out two rows of folding chairs with a few teens slouching on them. "They're the jury, nine of them," he whispers. They're watching me, so I wave to them. Penn pushes my arm down. The jury kids could care less.

Penn leads me to a table.

"The defense, that's us, sits here. Over there's the bailiff, the one who opened the door. And the kid with the laptop is the court reporter."

"What's the bailiff?"

"Assistant to the judge. The judge is the one in the black robe, the only grown-up in the room." She's got big, long hair pulled back, heavy eyebrows and small intense eyes. She spots Penn and grins like she's happy to see him. An American flag and a California State flag hang on poles behind her.

"Why's the bailiff in a cop suit?"

"There's a Police Academy Magnet High School here. Kids who want to be cops are part of that program."

"Why would anyone want to be a cop?"

"Just sit down and stay quiet."

The auditorium starts to fill up with other high school students. It's a lake of gray and black baggy t-shirts and hoodies. The students sign in at the front of the room and then find folding seats in the audience. They get extra credit to see me kicked around. Lucky them. Like some reality show, only there are no cameras.

And then I see the cop lady who arrested me. She's sitting at the back of the auditorium in her uniform. She catches my eye and winks. I'm guessing she didn't think I'd do it. Or did she?

Penn whispers: "You know how everybody always says when things get difficult, 'Just be yourself?' Well don't. Be respectful and try to behave."

Everyone is taking this so seriously. I really want to laugh, but Penn is so into it, I don't want to ruin it for him.

And I don't want to ruin it for the kid who's sketching me. He must be the courtroom artist. I like it when artists draw me. That's why I hang with Dakota; he's not my boyfriend, but people think we're hooking up but it's more like I'm his model and he's this really fly artist and he doesn't expect me to love him or crap like that.

Why is Penn grabbing me, pulling me up from my chair? Why is everybody standing?

"All rise," shouts the bailiff, glaring at me.

"You weren't listening," hisses Penn. "That was the third

time he said it."

"Face the flag of our country, recognizing the principles for which it stands," the bailiff drones. I look around and everybody is actually facing the flag. "The Venice Beach High School Teen Court is in session, the Honorable Samantha Mitchell, Judge, presiding. Please be seated and come to order."

Everybody sits and the judge nods in recognition.

"Will the defendant please rise?" The judge looks at me. So I stand.

"State your full name for the record," she asks.

"Kalifornia Blu Cooper." There are some snickers when the kids in the audience hear my real name. My mom thought Kalifornia was a radical name. Blu is her last name and Cooper is my dad's last name. They never thought what it would be like for me as a teenager. Most people call me Kal anyway. And I usually leave out the Cooper part. I'm just Kalifornia Blu, except when everything is all official like this.

"Ms. Cooper, you are here because you signed an agreement to have your case heard here at Teen Court rather than Juvenile Hall." She points to the jury kids. "This is the jury that is going to hear your trial. Is it still your desire to have your case heard at Teen Court?"

"Yes," I answer.

"I don't see a parent here."

I start to answer, but then Penn stands up and says, "Her mother is detained, your Honor."

"Penn, you know we can't conduct a trial without a parent attending. Ms. Cooper, is your mother stuck in traffic or is she not available today?"

"She'll be here, Judge," says Penn. "Right?" He turns to me.

Not a chance. I shrug.

"Ms. Cooper, your arrest has some serious consequences. And your sentence will only be accepted by the court when a parent signs off on it. I'm worried that your parents are not concerned with your whereabouts, and without them here there is not much I can do for you."

"Your Honor, can you give us some more time? Her mother is on her way," Penn says.

Penn is trying to help, but he has no idea that I have no idea where my mom is.

"Ms. Cooper, I'll give you until tomorrow morning to convince your parents to appear in my courtroom. At that time if they are not here, I will move your case from Teen Court and send you to Juvenile Court. Which could mean a trip to Juvenile Hall. Do you understand me?"

"What if I can't get my mom to show up?"

"Is your father available?"

"My dad? I haven't seen him since I was a kid."

"Eight o'clock tomorrow morning. With a parent."

Her gavel comes down hard.

Penn ushers me towards the auditorium door. The cop lady catches my eye and looks at me like she kinda feels bad for me that my mom didn't show up. Again. Sympathy from a cop. That has to be a first.

There's a water fountain just outside the door so I bend down for a drink. Penn leans over, hissing at me again.

"Get on your damn cell phone and call your mom like right now."

He needs to relax, so I roll my head around to face him, my face close to his, looking up into his soft brown eyes and I let a whole mouthful of water drip and bubble out of my mouth and down my chin and all over my front. It works: he's confused, laughing, trying not to, but laughing. Damn, if he weren't so cute it'd be easier to hate him. Anyway, he's relaxed enough to look into my eyes. He turns his head to get a better angle. "They're green. They were blue yesterday. What's the deal with your eyes?"

"Colored contact lens."

"Why have you got to change your eye color?"

"I get bored." His eyes linger on mine for just a second longer.

I think he realizes he's a bit close. He jumps back and starts walking.

"Abusing attorney client privileges?" I call after him.

"Call your mom," he yells back as he walks towards the parking lot.

"It's no use. She won't answer the phone." Why am I following him? I never follow anybody.

"Well, let me call her then. What's her number?" He pulls out his cell phone, still walking.

"She's not gonna show, Penn. Just forget about it."

"Maybe she got lost."

"She's not lost. She's gone."

He looks confused. "Gone where?"

"How do I know?"

"How is that possible? Didn't you tell her this was important?"

"I told her."

We stop in front of a silver Vespa. Old school. Not bad. And good timing: I want to change the subject.

"Why don't you give me a ride home since you suck as a lawyer?"

"Hey, I bought you more time."

"One day."

"Where do you live?"

"Santa Monica, on Ocean."

"Where?"

"You know the big building that kind of hangs off the cliff above PCH, near Chautauqua?"

"With all the balconies? Seriously?"

"Yeah."

"Awesome. Except there's no entrance. I've driven by a thousand times."

"Not from Pacific Coast Highway. Off the top of the cliff, onto the roof."

"For real?"

"There's a bridge over. I'll show you if you stop yakking and start riding."

"All right, hop on."

I strap my board to my backpack. He gets on the scooter. I slide on behind him.

"Hold on." I take that seriously and grab on tight, gripping his stomach.

"So I don't fall off."

Penn weaves his way through the disgusting afternoon traffic. I have to say, he's not a bad driver. My cell phone rings. Caller ID spells out: Devil. AKA: My mom. And god damn if she isn't all nice and innocent:

"How'd it go today?"

"Where are you?"

"Hawaii. Maui, actually. Oh it's so..."

"Maui!?" I yell at her, "You flake on me, I go to jail!"

"Oh, bean sprout, you're in jail?"

"I did what I had to do."

"What does that mean? It sounds very passive-aggressive. I'm sure Bernie can handle you. Anyway, my voice is kicking ass like you can't believe, bean, like a sonic wonderland, magical, but really real..."

I hang up.

"Your mom's in Maui?" Penn tries to turn his head to look at me but he swerves and barely gets the scooter back in control. We are headed up Ocean, where multi-million dollar condos stare smugly at the ocean. Well, they have to look through Palisades Park to see the Pacific, but that's just a narrow strip of joggers and old people being pushed along in wheelchairs. And it has some weird, cool, twisted trees. I try to climb them sometimes, but of course that's a misdemeanor and people shake their heads at me. The far side of the park is the cliff that drops down to Pacific Coast Highway and the beach. And at the far end of the park is my building, with its roof level with the top of the cliff.

I point Penn to the little bridge that leads onto the parking area on the roof. I swipe my card at the security gate but nothing happens. Then the valet, Lloyd, comes over and lifts the gate by hand. Lloyd glances at the old scooter and then at Penn. He raises an eyebrow at me.

"Hello, Ms. Blu. We're having some trouble with the gate. Should be fixed by tomorrow." He nods to Penn.

"I'm her lawyer."

Lloyd is very discreet; he merely raises his eyebrow a little higher and says: "Of course."

Penn rolls over to the all glass entryway with its all-glass elevator as Lloyd closes the gate behind us. I get off the Vespa.

"You need to get your mom on a plane," says Penn quietly.

"Yeah." My eyes swell up a little bit. I wipe my face with my sleeve. "It's just from the wind," I say quickly.

Penn starts to reply, stops himself. He's looking at me like he wants to hug me, but I'm probably projecting and I don't want a hug, I don't need a hug... it's just that I've sort of been hugging him the whole way on the scooter. Why's he staring at me? He snaps out of his trance. Me too.

"Don't be late tomorrow," he says. "The judge said eight o'clock. With your mom, or you're going to Juvie Hall." He guns his little scooter dramatically, zooms off... but has to stop quickly and wait for Lloyd to raise the security gate.

I watch Penn leave through the gate and feel entirely alone until Lloyd walks over to me and says, "Your mom's not coming back anytime soon, is she?"

"I can handle it." I turn and walk away from him and wonder if he has any clue what kind of deep shit I'm really in. I hate his watchful eye. Maybe I should just run away so nobody can look at me. Maybe I'll ride to the airport, lay down my credit card and get a ticket on the next flight to wherever. But instead I stand in front of my great glass elevator and wait for Lloyd to hit the button for me and hold the door open. He presses the tenth floor and I walk into the small glass box and the elevator door closes and I'm on my own.

Chapter Five

Gleeson is the closest thing to a friend that I have, even though she's twice my age. She lives next door to me and we tell each other everything. I don't really relate to kids my age; I have much more in common with Gleeson.

She has a two year-old kid named Stella that I watch sometimes when Gleeson's Pilates instructor comes to her apartment. She's got a whole Pilates set-up with big machines and ropes and handles and long metal springs. After the instructor leaves, Gleeson and I usually sit around and drink Chai tea and talk. I've just told her what happened. She doesn't look happy about it. She looks at me real serious.

"Don't go to jail."

"Not going to."

"Yeah, you are. Your mom's not coming home tonight, you know it."

"She's a bitch."

"I think she thinks her lawyer will save you. Bernie's gotten your mom out of worse holes than you're in now. So she's not too worried, that's all."

Gleeson used to be a punk rocker. I mean a real one, the

kind that lived in New York City in 1979 and spiked her hair with glue and asked tourists for money. She wears pretty cool clothes. Sometimes she hands-me-down a few. Right now she's wearing striped Betsy Johnson leggings and a Hello Kitty sweatshirt.

"I'm not calling her lawyers. I can deal with this myself. Bernie can go stroke and flatter my mom, but I don't need her. And I'm never dealing with her lap dog, Chandara, ever again."

"Okay, whatcha gonna do?"

"I've got a plan."

"Don't shoot anyone."

"Seriously, it can work."

"What's the plan?" I can tell she's getting impatient because she's putting her ankles into some sheepskin straps.

"I'll track down my dad. What do you think?"

"Radical, kiddo. How about that he's some violent, evil thug who abandoned you when you were eight? Any of that make any difference?" She's pulling on a rope that's yanking her legs up into the air.

"I don't have a lot of options."

"You got Bernie."

"I swore to Chandara I'm doing this myself. I can handle my father. I just need him to sign this court thing. No biggie."

"How the hell are you going to find him?" She walks her hands to the edge of the Pilates thingy and lets go. She's hanging completely upside down.

"I'll Google him."

Gleeson's sweatshirt falls over her face, revealing a weird, kind-of-radical pattern of scars around her belly button. I knew she used to scar herself when she was a punk and she showed me some on her arm. She calls it branding. But she never showed me this: diamond shapes and hexagons carved into her belly. So much cooler than tattoos. And super creepy.

"Can I use your computer?"

"Go ahead."

I sit at the desk and wake up her computer. Sometimes I wish Gleeson were my mom. She would totally have shown up at Teen Court today. I don't think she needs a baby sitter as much as she wants someone to hang out with. Her husband's a producer, always off somewhere making movies.

I've never Googled my dad before. Never needed to. Never crossed my mind. I type his name, Zachary Cooper, in the search box and hit Return.

5,263 results. The first is: Melanee Blu Biography. I open it and read to myself: "While playing in L.A. clubs, Melanee met singer-songwriter Zachary Cooper and they had their first child, Kalifornia Blu."

My mother is Melanee Blu–the recording artist. A long time ago, she was Melanee Blu–the rock star. She's having a comeback now. She thinks kids my age are listening to her. She has this sort of grunge whiney sound that was big in the early days. She had a couple of hits and sold lots of records but fell off the charts and hasn't had a hit since. She's even hosted MTV TLC. Embarrassing. Not like I ever watch that crap, but the kids in my school did. For about a week I was popular. Nobody knew who my mom was before then. It's not like she showed up at PTA meetings.

I go back to the Zachary Cooper search page. I click on "images" and up pop hundreds of pictures of my mom... none of Zachary.

I scan through the listings while Gleeson pulls herself down from the straps.

"Find anything?"

"Nothing recent. Just stuff about my mom. Oh, wait. Here's something, looks like he's a collector of found art. Whatever that means."

Gleeson moves over to the Pilates reformer, a padded box with springs and poles. She does her favorite exercise– Elephant. Hands and feet on the platform, then she pushes this rolling thing back and forth.

"Try the Yellow Pages. Do you think he still lives in Los Angeles?"

"Probably. Although my mom never let me see him after they split." I type his name in the Yellow Pages box and hit return. A listing pops up.

"There's one address in Venice on Pacific Avenue."

"See if there's a Google map."

I type in the address and change the map to Satellite view and the buildings render on the screen. "He's on Pacific and Windward Circle." Right near the Boardwalk and the Venice Skate Park.

"Which building is he in?" Gleeson asks.

"That Chinese restaurant building." I click on the plus sign to make the image bigger.

"Ping's Place? Love their orange-ginger chicken."

"I wonder if his place smells like Chinese food? My mom hates Chinese food." I get in as tight on the image as I can and study every detail. I look at the cars surrounding the building and I wonder if one of them is his. I can't believe my dad actually lives there.

"Are you sure that's really him, Kali? There could be other guys with the same name."

Gleeson is the only one I don't mind calling me Kali. Kali is the name of a Hindu Goddess. She's the Goddess of destruction. Gleeson sees her as the Goddess of self destruction, which she knows I'm inclined to.

"Oh, I'm sure it's the same guy."

"How are you sure?"

"He grew up in Venice. He probably never left. I bet he's been here all this time." I pick up a pen and copy the address onto my hand.

"Well, are you gonna call him?" Gleeson says.

"He won't do anything. Why would he?"

"He may be your only chance," she points out.

The baby starts crying.

"Kali?" Gleeson calls out to me.

But I'm not listening to Gleeson or the baby crying. I'm thinking about what it would be like to see my dad again. And how he really is my only chance. And before the baby lets out another wail, I'm out the door.

Chapter Six

I'm skating along a sidewalk with a building above–it's got columns along the curb holding it up. The columns have sculpted faces at the top and tonight they all seem to be watching me. It's the old original Venice, when some of the roads were canals and lakes. I look down at the address on my hand. I don't see it, but Ping's Place is right here and around the back there's a wooden staircase leading up to a door. Must be it. I walk up the stairs and knock on the door. There's no answer. I knock again. Nobody. I check the mailbox. There are phone and cable bills and a jury duty notice addressed to Zachary Cooper.

I take a bobby pin out of my hair. I pull off the plastic tip and straighten out the pin. Then I slide it into the lock and turn it to the right. I wiggle it around a little, then the lock pops. I open the door and slip inside, closing the door quickly behind me.

The room is large and very dark. Venetian blinds slice the light from the street lamps outside.

"Hello. Anybody here? Hello, um, Zachary?" I call out in case he's not into answering the door.

"Oh, shit." There's a kid on a swing, sitting there in the dark, staring at me. I'm so freaked out, but it's not moving and as I get closer I see it's just an old, beat up crash test dummy, with tape and markings and sensors built in.

I lunge at the dummy. "Boo."

Nearby I find an old ornate Victorian lamp and turn it on. A row of unpainted marionette dolls look blankly at me from a high shelf. What the hell is this place?

I turn on more lamps–all antiques. Old framed posters of magicians cover one wall. A moose head with a massive rack looms over a Madonna and Child wooden icon. Circus freak signs painted on wooden boards lean against a desk. A headless child mannequin rides a carousel horse by the window, seemingly galloping over a medical model of a woman with her skin removed to show her digestive tract. A magician's Saw-The-Lady-In-Half box acts as a table. Fake feet in high heels stick out of one end. There's a dirty plate on it and this week's LA Weekly.

At the far end of the room I find a framed photo on an old oak desk. It's the only personal thing here: Me and Zachary, riding horses at Griffith Park. I think I'm six, maybe seven. I pick up the photo and look closely at it so that I can remember him. Remember being there. I hold on to the photo.

It sounds like one of those talk radio programs is on, the voices coming from behind an old fancy carved Spanish door that's slightly ajar. Looking in, I see the end of an ancient four-poster bed. I open the door slowly, in case he's in there asleep. But the bed is empty. An Art Deco radio is chattering, I turn off the radio and sit on the bed. Guitars hang on the walls, floor to ceiling–dozens of them, electric, acoustic, twelve-string, every kind.

There's a note-pad shoved under the pillow. I can't really read it in the dim light coming in the window, but I can make out lyrics and music notations. Great. The only thing worse than lawyers is musicians. Everybody tells me my mom's not that bad, compared to so-and-so… And my mom always said there's no one worse than my dad…

I lie back on the bed, and wait.

Chapter Seven

Sunlight rips through the blinds. I'm still in Zachary's bedroom. I guess I fell asleep–which is weird, since I usually can't at night, but I guess I haven't slept in a couple of days. I crack my back and there's a strange sound, not just my back. It's the front door opening.

I hear footsteps. I slip off the bed and peek through the crack in the bedroom doorway.

There he is, my father: Zachary Cooper. It's kind of like looking at a ghost. Somebody I once knew who then was dead to me. But there he is. He's got long dirty blonde hair that's been bleached a little by the sun. He's really tan and his face is kind of weathered. I guess he's in his thirties like my mom. He takes off his tie and black suit jacket off and flops down on the sofa. He has really broad shoulders and looks super strong. He must work out a lot.

Now he's looking around. I think he just noticed the lamps are on. He gets up from the sofa and turns them off, seeming confused. Just then I bump the door and it creaks.

Zachary crouches behind a desk. "Stay where you are. I have a weapon." His voice is loud and intimidating. He sounds super mad and explosive. I recognize that voice from when I was a kid. It always scared me.

I watch as he reaches inside a drawer. Now he's slowly walking down the hallway towards me holding a gun. I better do something quick. At least say something.

"Wait, Zachary, it's me Kal."

He stops. "What?"

"Your daughter, Kalifornia."

I push the door open slowly with my foot. He's still holding the gun. I pull back my hair. We both freeze and look into each other's eyes. His eyes are blue, like mine. His hair is blonde, like mine, and he's got a bunch of earrings too, like mine. I can kind of make out a tattoo peeking out from under his shirt.

He takes a step closer, just a step. He brushes his hair out of his eyes. "Kali? My Kali?"

I can see the scar on his right cheek, a clean straight line that starts at his ear and tilts down towards his bottom lip. He's only a few feet away.

"I remember that scar," I say.

That's when I notice the gun is dripping water.

"It's a friggin' water pistol?"

He looks at it like it's poison and throws it on the couch.

"Oh, Kali, I'm…"

"It's Kal." I knew this was a bad idea. What was I thinking coming over here?

"You're all grown up." He's moving his arms up and out. Oh, no, is he thinking he's going to hug me? I duck under his arms. He's a lousy, irresponsible, screwed-up bastard. So hugging isn't what I really want to do right now. "How did you get in here? Is your mom here too?" He starts looking around for Melanee.

I ignore the questions and pull my cell out of my pocket to check the time. "It's seven forty-eight!" I panic. "Shit. We gotta go. Where's your ride?" I start towards the front door.

"Hold on. Wait," he yells. I turn around. "What the hell is going on? Did Melanee put you up to this?"

"No!" I squeal. "It has nothing to do with her." He's looking kind of freaked out right now. I don't think he expected me to ever show up.

"I know this is crazy me being here." My voice is a little crackly. "But I need your help. Please."

"Can you just slow down for a sec?" He leans on the desk. "Tell me what's going on. Start with that."

I shift a little from side to side then I look at my cell again. Maybe because it's almost eight or maybe 'cause I am looking at my dad for the first time in like years and need his help 'cause if I don't get it I might end up in jail. For whatever reason I freak and say, "There's no time. Come on, come on, come on!" I grab his tie and jacket that he left on the sofa and I'm out of the front door super fast, hoping he's following me.

Chapter Eight

"Don't you have a driver for this thing?" We're riding in a big, black stretch limo. Not the first time for me, but the first time in the front seat. He's driving.

"I'm the driver."

"You're a limo driver?"

"Yes, indeed I am. I am a limo driver." He looks like he's been up all night. He keeps turning towards me and staring. Like he can't believe what he's seeing.

"Watch the road," I point. He swerves back into his lane.

"How old are you?"

"Fifteen."

"That explains it."

"Explains what?" I ask.

"You, how you look... different."

"What did you expect?"

"How is your mom?"

"Fine."

"Chatty, aren't you?"

"Yeah." What's he want, Oprah?

Venice Beach High School is right down the street so it

doesn't take us long. The school is famous for being used as Rydell High School in the movie Grease. There the kids were dressed in colorful poodle skirts and bouncy ponytails. Today it's all dark pants and dark hoodies. The kids would be scowling if that wasn't so much effort. Nobody on this campus looks like they are about to burst into song. Unless zombies who have stayed up all night playing video games ever spontaneously burst into song. A few zombie heads swivel to stare at the limo.

"Just park right here, in front."

Zachary scrunches up his face, his wrinkles suddenly deep and long. "You want to get me towed?"

"You won't be here long enough to get a ticket."

"They charge you more for a limo."

The school bell rings. The kids drift towards the buildings.

"C'mon, c'mon, c'mon." I hate begging but this guy is not moving at all.

I slide out of the limo, waving at him to follow. He finally gets out, yelling loudly at me: "I'm not your dog." Great, about a hundred people heard that. Should I tell him if I ever got a dog it wouldn't be some stubborn, wrinkled old pit bull with earrings and an attitude?

Penn meets us by the cafeteria entrance. He's looking sharp in his suit. His face, however, is a confused mix of relief and exasperation.

"You're late. Where's your mom? You almost missed it." He notices Zachary. "Who's this?" he asks.

"Zachary Cooper, my father." Penn doesn't believe me, so I add, "Really. And this is Penn, Zachary."

Penn holds out his hand. "Nice to meet you, sir. Penn

Roth."

They shake. Penn is momentarily speechless. But he recovers quickly.

"The judge will be relieved to see you. I'm representing Kal in court today as her attorney." Penn sees I'm holding Zachary's coat and tie. He takes it from me and holds the coat open for Zachary to put on.

"Judge?" Zachary pushes the coat away. "Are you kidding me?"

"I'm sure Kal filled you in on what's going on."

"Actually, Penn, Kal hasn't told me a damn thing. And how old are you?"

This conversation isn't working; I need to move things along. "I got arrested, Zachary, no biggie. Gotta meet with the judge. Gotta go to pretend court, Teen Court. Must bring a parent. Just do what the judge tells you. You're my dad, that's the important thing to remember and you have to sign some papers, okay?"

"Slow down, Kali," says Zachary. "Where's your mom?"

"That's the point, she didn't show up. That's why I need you."

"I don't do courts and cops and judges, not when your mother is involved. Never works out. Just not my thing." He turns to walk away.

"Mr. Cooper," Penn steps in front of him, "without your help, Kalifornia could go to jail. We just need you to sign off on her paper work, then you can go."

"Yeah," I say, glaring at Zachary, "Tomorrow you can pretend you never even saw me. I'll leave you alone, if that's what you're worried about. And Melanee doesn't have to know anything about this."

The school bell rings. Zachary watches a teen cop open the double doors to the Auditorium.

"Are you two kidding me? Kid lawyers and now kid cops? What's going on? Am I being Punk'd or some shit?" He's looking around and up at the ceiling. "Are there cameras?"

"Teen Court is a program for teens who have committed a misdemeanor," Penn tries to explain. "A jury, a jury of their peers recommends a sentence. Kal has six months to carry out the sentence, and if completed successfully, her record is wiped clean."

"This is for real?"

I nod as Penn says, "It's real. The idea is to interrupt developing patterns of criminal behavior in juveniles."

"She's a developing criminal?"

"They're offering her a second chance."

"What'd you do?" Zackary asks me.

"Trespassing," I tell him.

"Where?"

I guess I have to get into the details. "Venice skate park, middle of the night."

"That's a crime?"

"Misdemeanor," says Penn. "But resisting arrest is more serious. The officers are willing to drop that charge if she attends Teen Court. It's a generous offer."

Zachary takes a deep breath, like he's hungry for air.

"Then Melanee flaked so you had to find me?" he asks.

"Umhum. So, are you going to help me?"

"Why not roll out the Big Guns?"

"Screw them. I can take care of it myself. But I need a

parent to sign off."

"A parent," Zachary snorts, like it's something smelly.

"Big Guns?" says Penn.

"Lawyers, real lawyers," snaps Zachary.

"Look, nobody's forcing you–"

But Penn interrupts me.

"Here at Venice Beach High School, we have a law magnet for kids who want to be lawyers. I'm in the law program and am assigned as Kal's legal counsel."

"You're just a kid."

"I'm sixteen."

"And this is legal and official?"

"It is both legal and official," says Penn, quite confidently, holding the jacket open again for Zachary.

For some reason this amuses Zachary. With a small sigh he slides into the jacket, throws the tie around his neck and starts tying it. "I never trusted those Big Guns either. Let's go," he says.

Chapter Nine

Penn, is your client's parent here today?" Judge Mitchell asks.

"Yes, your Honor, I'm here." Zachary stands up. Penn tugs on his jacket to sit down. He looks so out of place among these teenagers.

"Very well, we can proceed. Bailiff, please swear Kalifornia in."

The geeky looking kid in the cop uniform comes over and stands in front of me.

"Raise your right hand," he says, and I do. "Do you solemnly swear that the testimony that you are about to give in the matter now pending before this court will be the whole truth and nothing but the truth, so help you God?"

I say, "yes," even though I'm thinking, what's that actually mean? Is that even English: 'so help you God?'

The bailiff then goes on to explain that I have been arrested for trespassing on public property after dark. The jury listens carefully, and then the judge asks me how I plead. Penn has already advised me to say I'm guilty, so I do. And also because, well, I am.

The jury empties into another room for a while to figure out a torture for me. Zachary shifts around in his seat.

"A RING-DING DINGITY DING." Zachary's cell phone goes off suddenly and loudly. He reaches into his pants to dig it out and as he pulls it out the tone gets louder. "A RING-DING DINGITY DING." The kids in the audience crack up. Penn rolls his eyes and the judge does not look impressed.

"Sorry. Forgot to turn it off," he says also too loudly as he pockets the phone. He leans over to me and whispers, "I went to high school here. This is pretty weird for me."

"Well, it's pretty weird for me too."

The jury comes back into the room and the judge addresses them.

"Members of the jury, have you reached a verdict?"

The jury sings out, like a carefully rehearsed choir. "Yes, your Honor."

The judge asks, "Will the foreperson please state her name for the record?"

A sixteen-year old girl stands. Girl scout, cheerleader and a big smile like fingernails on chalkboard to me, though highly useful for a future trophy wife.

"Amber Morgan."

"Ms. Morgan, please read the sentence."

Amber smiles: "Your Honor, we the jury issue the defendant Kalifornia Blu Cooper to a curfew of 6:00 P.M. to 6:00 A.M. restricting her to home and school unless accompanied by a parent."

"You've got to be kidding!" I burst out. Penn tries to keep me quiet. The audience laughs and the judge bangs her gavel.

"Kalifornia?" asks the judge. "Who do you live with?"

"My mother."

"Is your mother at home now?"

"She's sick." Which is not altogether a lie, because she is totally sick as far as I am concerned. And I didn't say she's at home sick. But this judge is a hard-ass.

"Kalifornia, I should make you answer the question and be found in contempt, but I'll spare us the bother and remind you that your mother is in Hawaii and everybody who can search the Internet knows it." The judge puts on a pair of glasses reads from her laptop. "According to TMZ this morning *'recording artist Melanee Blu was cited with misdemeanor exposure for going topless on a public beach yesterday.'*" The judge takes a long moment, waiting for this to sink in and then she turns the knife, the sadist: "Seems she's just like you, and you're just like her. Except she's very talented."

There are snickers and ooohhhs from the audience. The judge bangs her gavel.

I look over at Zachary and he is just melting. Maybe from the heat or maybe from the shame of leaving me with my mistake of a mother for the last seven years.

"Who bailed you out the night of your arrest?" asks the judge.

"My mother's lawyer's assistant," I tell her.

"And your mother was where?"

"On a plane." I'm starting to feel hot now.

"Yesterday you said you hadn't seen your father since you were eight. Is that correct?"

"Yes," I say.

"That's right, your Honor. Her mother won sole custody," Zachary announces.

"I am also figuring your mother won't exactly be home tonight. Or tomorrow." Smart lady. "Who do you stay with when your mother is out of town?"

"My mom always has someone there with me at night."

Even as I say it, I know my answer sounds like a total lie. When I was little I had a series of groupie baby-sitters who watched me. My mom likes to surround herself with people who think she's cool, so she always had these girls around to take care of me. They'd eventually start stealing from her, or screw one of her boyfriends and she'd get rid of them. Now when my mom goes away, I stay home and I'm on my own. My choice. I can't stand those ratty girls telling me to brush my teeth.

"Mr. Cooper, are you aware of your daughter's living situation?"

"I haven't been, no, not till now."

"Mr. Cooper, do you have full time employment?"

"Yes, I drive a limo for a living."

"Are you a resident of Los Angeles?"

"I live in Venice."

"And are you currently under court supervision?"

"No, I'm not. Not for the past five years." He looks at me to see my reaction. Like I should be proud of him for not having been arrested for the past five years.

"Well, until her mother can make her way back to Los Angeles, I'm making you Kalifornia's temporary guardian."

"Him!?"

"Lower your voice, Kalifornia," the judge snarls. "Mr. Cooper?"

"Your Honor, I've been estranged from my daughter for

the past six years."

"Seven," I say under my breath.

She turns to me. "Kalifornia, it says here that you've attended five private schools in the past six years. Why so many?"

"We moved around a lot." Or I'd get kicked out because my mom would piss off the admin. Or I got caught doing... various things.

"I made a couple of calls and found that you aren't regularly attending classes in your current school. Is that right?" I shrug. "But I also found out you make decent grades when you do show up." I nod and half listen as I concentrate on how the silver pen she's fingering catches the sun.

"Kalifornia, I'm going to do something unconventional here and make it a requirement as part of your sentence that you transfer to Venice Beach High. And I am going to request that you transfer into the Police Academy Magnet for the duration of your six-month sentence, beginning today. I'd like to keep my eye on you."

"Cop school!?" Too loud again.

"Yes, cop school. It's fully your choice whether or not you participate in the Teen Court sentence. But if you decide not to, I'm going to transfer your case to Juvenile Court. Now Mr. Cooper, I think you will agree with me that your daughter could use a little looking after and perhaps a little discipline. You lost custody of your only child. A court clearly saw you as unfit. Would you say you are still unfit?"

I look over at Zachary: he seems like a fish out of water, or maybe a fish on the grill. "No, your Honor. I am fit. My situation is drastically improved but I'm still not certain..."

Penn jumps in: "Your Honor, is there a precedent for this, to sentence her to another school?"

"Probably not, but this is my courtroom and I'm making a deal with your client. This is the deal I'm presenting. What do you say, Ms. Cooper? Cop School or not?"

I look at Penn. He seems to be thinking about it. He's kinda cute when he's so serious. "I'd recommend taking the offer," he whispers, his warm breath on my neck.

I look at my cell phone vibrating in my lap. The caller ID tells me it's my mom, so I ignore it. But it makes me think: If I join the cop school, it'll really piss her off. If there's one thing she hates more than Chinese food, it's cops. Also, no one will ever think I'm anything like her.

"Yes, your Honor, I'll do it." So I say yes and go up to the judge's table and sign the damn papers that she thrusts at me.

I'm sure the judge thinks she's just won something but I won't give her the satisfaction of being scared or pissed or anything she's expecting. I stare at her, standing straight, like she hasn't hurt me. It's just six months; I can do anything for that long. Actually, up close, she doesn't seem smug. She's quite still, watching me. Her eyes seem almost kind. For a judge, she seems not judgmental at all. Weird. I rub my finger over the silver pen. It has turquoise embedded in it. It looks very old.

"Kalifornia," she says, "could I have my pen back?"

I almost drop it; I'm so surprised I'm still holding it. I hand it to her and she almost smiles. She hands it to Zachary and points to where he needs to sign.

I stare at the paper. Of course he doesn't want to do this.

The judge leans back and looks at him. "Mr. Cooper, Teen

Court offers teens a second chance. And today, I am offering you a second chance at fatherhood. We don't get many second chances in life."

Zachary flinches, like he's screwing up his courage, and it hurts.

"Yeah, I get it, Judge." He signs the papers.

The judge hands me a yellow slip of paper that says "Tardy" on it. "Find your way to the gymnasium and see Officer Mendoza. I'll put in the transfer papers from your old school today."

The bell rings.

"Good luck, Kalifornia and good luck, Zachary. I'll see you both back here in three months for Kal's first assessment."

The judge bangs her gavel and the auditorium empties.

I guess Penn is in Judge Mitchell's law class 'cause the two of them walk out the door chatting about Brown vs. The Board of Education.

I start to leave the room. Zachary catches up with me. "Hey. You mind telling me what this is all about?"

"Just show up here in three months like the judge says. I'll be okay."

Zachary's not happy. "Woof woof! Fetch. Don't drool on me. That's about it?"

"Pretty much." We are outside now, squinting in the bright sunlight.

"After seven years..."

"Do you want me to thank you?" Cold, I know, but I don't know what he's after and I don't want to find out.

"No, it's not that. The judge just said you have to move in with me."

Is he serious?

"Yeah, like that's going to happen," I say. "I'll be fine."

"And if I change my mind?" He's talking in a quiet snarl.

"You can't. You just signed."

"I can tell the judge why and how I lost custody."

"Then I go to jail." Is he even trying to understand?

The second bell rings.

"Give me your hand," he says.

"What?"

"It's at the end of your arm. Take your time finding it." I slowly hold out my right hand thinking he's going to shake it. Instead he takes the silver pen from the judge's table out of his pocket and writes his phone number on the inside of my palm.

"Now, what's yours?" I roll my eyes, give him my digits and watch him write them on the inside of his hand. He hands me the pen. I stick it in my pocket, not really thinking.

Zachary starts running away. Of course. What's odd is how fast he's running, like a sprinter, or like he's being chased by dogs. But then I realize there's a parking enforcement person circling his limo.

Chapter Ten

Balancing on my tiptoes I look through a small square wire mesh window on the gymnasium door. Forty kids, mostly boys, in full police uniform, stand in straight rows like soldiers. The bailiff from Teen Court struts between the lines, inspecting, trying to look fierce.

There's no teacher around so I could probably just ditch. Right now I'm doubting my decision and wondering just how important that night ride was. I can still feel that warm breeze and hear the roar of the waves.

"We were expecting you, Ms. Cooper." Holy shit, I spin round and there's a real cop standing over me. He doesn't try to look fierce; he *is* fierce, though in a quiet, still way.

"I'm Officer Julio Mendoza. Come on inside." He holds the door open for me and I walk into the gym. He's wearing a full LAPD uniform complete with a freakin' gun.

The bailiff shouts: "Attention." The kids stand up straight with their left arm at their side and their right hand at their forehead–saluting. All their feet are in the same position, resembling a ballet dancer's first position. They wear light blue short-sleeved polo shirts and dark blue pants. The boys all have short-cropped hair and the few girls all have their hair pulled back into a bun.

Officer Mendoza looks them over. He nods to the bailiff who says, "At ease." Together, they separate their feet a bit and put their hands behind their backs like a well-rehearsed dance.

"Cooper, get over here." He looks at me.

I walk across the gym. All eyes are watching me and they don't seem friendly or supportive. I'm pulling my best tough-ass face. So what ... they all are.

"This is Kalifornia Cooper. She's been sentenced to join us by Teen Court. She may find it hard to fit in this program."

No shit, I'm thinking.

"I want you to try extra hard to make her fit in." I don't like the way he says 'make her.' Two of the girls giggle. He sounds like the lead hyena barking to the pack to move in on the kill.

"Jade," Mendoza calls out.

A skinny Chinese girl answers, "Sir, yes, sir."

"You're going to be Kalifornia's partner. Help her get outfitted. The rest of you..." he pauses and his voice rises to shout, "are you ready for physical fitness?"

They all call out in unison, "Sir, yes, sir."

Is this for real?

So, now this Jade slinks to the front of the line. She's not too pleased with her new assignment, I can tell. Maybe she was out of line, and I'm the punishment. She sure behaves like I am.

Mendoza tosses Jade a clear plastic bag full of clothes. She takes off with the bag and Mendoza does this little head tilt in my direction which I guess means I should follow her.

Without saying a word, Jade leads me into the girl's locker room. And then as hard as she can, she heaves the plastic bag at me. Charming.

She glares at the mirror and picks lint off her uniform. I take the bag into a toilet stall.

Inside the bag is a light blue polo shirt with a police badge sewn above the pocket. The badge reads: Preparing to Serve, Law Enforcement Magnet School. The word "Student" is embroidered at the top. There's also a pair of blue khaki pants, and a blue pullover sweatshirt without a hood. The sweatshirt actually says POLICE on the back of it. Like I'm ever gonna wear that. I put on the shirt and pants and ditch the sweatshirt behind the toilet. I shove my clothes in the bag. Then I unzip my new khaki's and pee.

"How'd you end up in this program?" I call from the stall.

There's a long pause, like she's trying to ignore me. So I open the stall door. She didn't expect to watch me pee and stares in disbelief. At least now she answers the question.

"I've wanted to be a cop since I could walk."

"You've got to be kidding?"

She's re-doing her long black ponytail, her back turned, ignoring me again.

"We're partners. What's that mean?"

"It means I have to spend a lot of time with you," she snaps. She pins her hair back into a bun.

"Lucky you." I finish peeing, zip up my pants and flush the toilet. She turns to face me. I may be kidding myself, but I think she appreciates it that I'm not shy with her.

"Better watch your ass, girl," she growls. "You don't know

what you've gotten yourself into."

"Is that a threat?"

"It's the truth." She starts to leave then turns back to me. "Tie your hair back. Has to be out of your face or you won't pass inspection." She drops a rubber band on the sink.

She's gone. I move towards the sink. I tie my dreadlocks back into a ponytail with the rubber band. I hate being told what to do. God, I will die if anyone I know sees me wearing a cop uniform. I turn to a full-length mirror mounted on a wall and stare at myself in this hideous outfit. Not even believing this is happening.

Chapter Eleven

So far, cop school is just like gym class. Luckily I can usually hold my own with the jocks. So here I am shimmying up a rope hanging over the basketball court next to Jade. She keeps giving me that look–like she's trying to psych me out, but I throw it right back at her. She hits the top first, but I make it to the top a second later. How about that, *sir?*

Mendoza tries to hide his surprise.

Next we stand on grimy gray gymnastic mats facing our partners.

"Jade, Kalifornia, I want you two to demonstrate how to get out of a back arm-lock. Jade, stand behind her and wrap your arms around her. Not too tight."

She does and seems to get great pleasure from squeezing the air out of me. Mendoza continues to blab about something else as Jade pulls tighter. No way am I gonna let this little bitch get away with that. So I cross my hands in front of me and throw them down towards the ground, at the same time I push my pelvis backwards as hard as I can. The force throws Jade from me and she misses the mat, landing on the hardwood floor.

Jade's just lying there on her back when the bell rings. Mendoza gives her a hand up. She's not happy.

"Go on, Jade. Hit the lockers."

He turns to me. "Where'd you learn that move, young lady?"

"Saw it in a Peter Konrad movie." I'm guessing Mendoza didn't think the reference was funny, but at least it was true.

"After Nutrition, go to the admin office to pick up your schedule. They'll give you a map of the school. And check the attitude. It's not welcome here."

Check my attitude? I don't even want to be here.

You can't even imagine what it's like to walk down the halls of a high school with a cop uniform on. The cop program has about 200 kids. There are like 2,000 kids in this school. So I stick out like I'm the only one who didn't get the memo not to wear your Halloween costume to school today.

I find the snack bar, buy some Cheetos and then walk down to the admin office. That's some way over-colored food product I'm swallowing. The lady at the admin desk hands me a Xeroxed map of the campus and a freshman Police Academy Magnet Schedule. I open today's schedule and read:

Wednesday
First Period–Inspection/Physical Training
Nutrition
Second Period–Biological & Forensics Science
Third Period–Computer/ Legal Communication
Lunch
Fourth Period–English
Fifth Period–Algebra

Sixth Period–Foreign Language/ Law

I'm walking down the hall studying the schedule. Algebra–fifth period. I didn't realize cops had to be good at math. What do they do, besides add up how many kids they arrest every day?

That's when I notice Mendoza in the judge's office, talking. The door is open so I stop outside for a sec and listen.

"I heard that she held her own in physical fitness today," the judge says.

"I don't care how she does. I don't want her in my program. Kids who want to be cops are desperate to participate. Do you want me to tell their parents I'm putting a criminal in their kid's spot?"

"Your precious cadets aren't all saints."

"They will be when I'm done with them."

"Saints with guns? Look, if I remember correctly, Julio, you weren't a saint either at their age. Didn't someone give you a second chance?"

"And your point is?" snaps Mendoza.

"The way I see it, it's a win-win situation for both of us. I'm thinking of a major expansion of your excellent program. Tomorrow I'm having dinner with some of the school board and I'm going to put a word in for you."

Mendoza is silent. "I think you're beginning to see my point." Mitchell is speaking quietly and I can barely hear her.

"Samantha, you're a slick weasel and I mean that…"

"As a compliment, I know. And that's how I take it."

"Thanks for your confidence in my program," Mendoza says.

"Good luck with the turning-Kalifornia-into-a-saint thing," says Mitchell with a chuckle.

So now they're laughing at me. Footsteps. He's coming out. I flee down a side corridor. I hear his footsteps, but I'm not looking back. I learned my lesson; who says I'm not a good student? I duck around a corner and out the building. Good, lots of kids. I slow down, all calm, innocent, lost in the crowd.

Chapter Twelve

I usually hate going home, but after one day in cop school, all I want to do is dump this uniform and sit in the Jacuzzi. I can see the pool area from the glass elevator as I descend to my floor. Good, there's no one in the hot tub.

You can only get to two apartments on my floor from this elevator: Gleeson's and mine. Very private... except of course that a million people driving down Pacific Coast Highway can practically see into my apartment. But they don't... but if they did, if they saw some of the stuff my mom gets into with her friends, sometimes right out here on the balcony, let's just say there'd be some major pile-ups on PCH. Actually, some of the neighbors down in the canyon have complained a few times, "You know, for the children, they shouldn't have to see such behavior..." Yeah, well how about me? Seeing it up close and personal my whole life. That sounds like I'm complaining, but I'm not.

It's kinda weird to live in an apartment. Everybody I know lives in houses in LA. I think my mom likes apartments 'cause it makes her feel like she's in a hotel and constantly on tour. I only ever lived in a real house once when I was a kid when we lived with Zachary.

My bedroom is down the hall next to my mom's. There's a huge window in my room that leads to another balcony with my mattress on it. That's where I sleep. I throw a tarp over when it rains, so I sleep there even in a storm. I just hate being cooped up inside.

The rest of the apartment is filled with my mom's crap: instruments, clothes... more instruments. Actually, that's all there is: instruments and clothes. I dragged a drum kit into my room, which is partly why my mattress is outside–there's not enough room for a bed anymore anyway.

I walk into the foyer, a long hallway that leads into the living room. I tear off the police shirt. I want to rip it, but I know I have to wear it tomorrow. I stand in front of the full-length hallway mirror and examine myself. I pinch my stomach, alert for fat. I look awful. No I don't. I just don't look like a super model. Then, of course, neither do the models. I've got a million dollar idea: full length mirrors that Photoshop you in real time. Awesome.

I take off the blue khakis, pull on my jeans and a Simple tank top from the clean laundry bag that the concierge dropped off and head into the kitchen to see if there is something cold to drink. It's through the living room. I almost scream.

When my mom started recording in here she had a giant clear Plexiglas soundproof box built around and over and under a grand piano. It looks pretty trippy, though I'm used to it. But I'm not used to seeing Zachary in the Plexi box, playing the friggin' grand piano.

It's sound proof so he can't hear me yelling at him. I bang my fists on the Plexi wall to get his attention. He looks up like he's seeing a ghost. I yank open the door as he spins around on the bench.

"What the hell are you doing here?" I yell. "You effing broke into my apartment?"

"You broke into mine." Real smooth.

"You haven't seen me in seven years and that's the best you can say?" I ask.

I turn my back on him and walk into the kitchen, which is a mess from takeout containers and old pizza boxes. My mom hates maid service, so our place is always a mess. She doesn't let anyone clean it. And don't think she's gonna clean it. I usually take the trash out, but it's been a busy week.

"It looks like your mom's been in Hawaii for a while."

"Are you spying on me?"

"Do you want to talk about it?"

"It's none of your damn business," I tell him.

"The judge thinks it is my business."

"I don't need your help anymore. Thank you." There, I thanked him. I move past him down the hallway towards the front door.

"You can't live alone. You're fourteen."

I stop dead in my tracks.

"F-I-F-T-E-E-N," I yell and spell.

His voice goes real soft, "Listen, Kali."

He forgets so easily. "It's Kal." I pull on my checkerboard Vans and pick up my skateboard.

I hold the front door open. "Get out of my apartment."

He hesitates then brushes past me into the hallway. I drop my skateboard and wheel into the hall, slamming the door behind me. I make a point to double bolt it.

"So, how have you been?" Now he's making small talk?

"Health-wise–excellent."

He doesn't like that snarky answer I guess. I lean on the elevator button.

"Don't you get it? You're in a lot of trouble. This court shit can screw up your life. It can affect you going to college or getting a job…"

"Like my life isn't screwed up already?"

It's like he stopped breathing. Good. Maybe he'll finally leave me alone.

This elevator is damn slow coming.

"Your mom on tour?"

"Prepping for one."

"She's got a radiant voice."

"I'll be sure and tell her."

"Don't sneer at me. I mean it."

Here's the elevator. Finally. He follows me inside.

"When's the last time you saw her?"

I hit the lobby button and slump against the wall and look out to the pool below. "I don't know, Labor Day?"

That sets him off. "Four weeks ago?"

"I used to travel with her, but I stopped because we just fought all the time." I can see Gleeson and Stella playing in the shallow end of the pool.

"What did you fight about?"

I watch the pool. "Men mostly."

He seems surprised.

Then I say, "Sometimes, we fight about you."

"Me?"

"She says you ruined her life."

"And you disagree?"

"Well, way back when, you really pissed her off." The elevator door opens. "It doesn't matter anyway. I'm too old to pretend I have a functional family." I throw down my board and skate into the lobby.

He jogs alongside me through the lobby and the parking lot. The garage gate is open; some workmen are fixing it. Zachary just stands there outside and watches as I roll down the up ramp, off the curb and out into traffic.

I grab onto the fender of a passing taxicab and squat down low. Skitching. It's all about watching the street, watching for holes, and trash and shit... but I gotta glance back. As I thought, he's come out to the sidewalk and is still watching me.

Drop it, Zachary. I'm gone. I'm not going to change your life. I'm not even in your life. How come I can't remember to not look back? It gets me in trouble every time. Have to look forward, look down; focus on the road.

Chapter Thirteen

It's almost dark. I skate my way down Ocean Avenue, hanging a right on a street called Fraser. Dakota's house is a big old Victorian about half way down the one-way street. I pop off my board and head into the house. The door is open as usual, so I let myself in and head upstairs to his bedroom. Dakota is shirtless, kneeling on the floor in his black H&M boxers. He's using a stinky tube of white shoe polish, the kind with the spongy top, to write on his black jeans, which he's stuffed and spread out like they're part of a dead body. Dakota's mom is a costume designer for the movies, so since he was a kid Dakota has been making his own clothes. That, and he's a junior at a Waldorf school in the Valley where they teach you to knit and sew.

I bend down and kiss his tan back.

"Hey, kitty-cat," he mumbles. "Rad, huh?" I lean on top of him and check out his work.

He's painted words and punk rock symbols all over the skinny jeans. The white shoe polish really pops on the black pants. He's also attached safety pins all down the right side of one leg. He always has safety pins on some part of his clothes.

He spins around, making me slip off his back onto the floor. He climbs on top of me.

"Let's do you next." He pulls off my shoestring belt and starts to unbutton my jeans. He's not ever too romantic, but this is ridiculous.

"Hey, slow down." But he's already pulled off my pants. Then next thing I know he's lying on top of my pants instead of me, and stuffing them with the rags. When he gets them nice and filled out, he starts drawing really intricate patterns, like tattoos, with a White-out pen. It looks cool, but I realize it's gonna take him a while, so I jump into his bed and pick up a Thrasher Magazine.

"Your mom home?"

"Nope. She's working on some Robert Pattinson movie. Went to Boston this morning." He rolls my jeans over and starts sketching on the butt.

"Can I sleep over?"

"Yeah, sure." He doesn't look up. He's so into his work, into his art, into my jeans, he couldn't care less about me or whether I'm staying over.

I snuggle under the covers with the magazine and wait for him. Jealous of my jeans.

Chapter Fourteen

My phone is ringing. I reach over to the bedside table and grab it.

"Hello?"

No one's on the other end but it keeps ringing.

"You answered mine. What time is it?" Dakota asks sleepily.

I look at the clock on his phone.

"It's almost six."

I put down Dakota's phone and I dive for my jeans. They're still stuffed, and they look wicked. Dakota must have worked on them all night. But no phone in the pocket. I scramble around on the floor, looking. I guess we didn't get busy; I don't even remember him getting into bed. There's my phone, by the door, still ringing.

"Hello."

"Kal, where are you?"

"Who is this?"

"It's Zachary. At your apartment. You aren't here. I guess you know that. This custody-curfew is tough enough without you..."

"Get out of my apartment."

"You're breaking the law."

"Arrest me, then."

"Are you okay?

"What do you care?"

That stops him. Silence. I don't have time to listen to silence. I should hang up. But then he starts talking again.

"Can you get to school from where you are? You are going to school today?"

"Yes." Jeez, so many questions.

"On time?"

"Well, maybe if I wasn't on the phone with you all day"

"Kali, back off. I'm in big trouble if I don't watch you. I got a shitload of paper work about this custody thing and it says–"

"That's not my problem."

"Yeah, it is." It's way too early for all this.

"Meet me after school," he says.

"Fine." Why did I just agree to that?

"Come to my apartment."

"Yeah, okay." There I go agreeing again. "Can I go now?"

"After school then."

"Yeah, later."

I hang up the phone. Dakota is watching me.

"What was that?" he asks.

"My dad. I'm supposed to move in with him. Some court shit."

He sits up, all interested. "I didn't even know you had a dad."

"I haven't seen him since I was like eight."

"No shit? That is the raddest. Can I meet him?"

"No! I don't want to have anything to do with him. Why would you want to meet him?"

Dakota looks a bit hurt and turns over. That was a little mean of me. Dakota doesn't have a dad either. His mom is a lesbian and she had him with some designer sperm she picked out of a catalogue. She showed me the guy in the catalogue, a burly football dude. Dakota doesn't look anything like him, so I think they cheated her, or there was some mix-up.

"I gotta go. I'll text you later. Okay?"

He kind of grunts.

I pull on my jeans, which still stink of White-out and shoe polish. The last thing I want to do is go home and put on that lame cop uniform. Especially with Zachary bugging me about it, sounding all like he really cares. It's bullshit. Couldn't he have called me even once all these years? How about not totally disappearing? Maybe fight for custody or something? Nothing; he just goes off and gets on with his own life. I'm not saying it's a big deal. It's not like I care. But I found *him*, not the other way around.

Chapter Fifteen

My second day of cop school and I'm gonna be late. Mendoza says I'm late three times I'm out of the program–which would be great except then I'd break my contract with Teen Court which means off to Juvenile Court and blah, blah, blah. At least I have my uniform on. Bad news is I look like a total geek. Worse than geek, a dork. Worse than a dork: a Po-Po.

The forensics class is meeting outside today. They're all hunched over in the back parking lot looking at something on the ground. Oh shit, it's a body. It's that girl Jade, my partner. Her head is bashed in and it looks like she's in a coma. Why are all these idiots just standing around? I run up, freaked out and the class all look at me like I'm crazy and I'm thinking they are super crazy ignoring Jade... then Jade scratches herself and the whole class cracks up. Laughing at me. I haven't been laughed at like that in a long time. And I can't fight back, since they're right and I'm the idiot. Mendoza frowns at me but turns to Jade.

"Young lady," he growls at Jade, "you're dead. The dead don't scratch." Everyone thinks that is really funny. Okay now

I get it. It's a crime scene and Jade is the victim. Pinch me, I really am in cop school.

Mendoza tells the class to settle down and they reluctantly go back to examining the crime scene. Most of them seem to be staring at Jade, like she's going to tell them the answer. One girl photographs her. A boy gets down on all fours and sniffs her. Another boy tugs at her socks, looking at her ankle. Glad I'm not the victim.

"Don't touch the body!" barks Mendoza. "Cooper," oh, no, now Mendoza is barking at me now. "You get an automatic 'F' for today's forensic quiz. I have zero tolerance for lateness."

A tall, athletic African-American girl named Keeba shakes her head at me. Already I can tell she's one of those over-achiever types. I'm getting the feeling most of these kids are. I'm the only one who didn't want to join in on the fun. They can tell, too.

Mendoza stands over Javier, a shy Hispanic kid, and says, "Okay, young man, what did you find?"

Javier reads from a notepad: "Lacerations to the back of the head. Blunt instrument trauma. Murder? Possible motive: theft."

"What theft? What's missing?"

"I was just thinking," Javier shrugs.

"No, that's what you *weren't* doing."

"Yes, sir."

"Evidence. Ever heard of it? See any? Get it together, detectives!" He glares over at me and shouts: "Cooper, get in there. Move it."

I'm tired of his attitude. "You failed me already. What's the point?"

"What's the point, *Sir*?" says Mendoza. "You're a loser, Cooper. You know what a loser is? Someone who thinks they're a loser. Like you do, Cooper." Why is he talking so quietly now? Everybody can still hear him, and they're enjoying it, smirking to each other. Mendoza's done with me, I guess, because he turns his back and walks off, not even waiting for the required 'Yes, sir.'

"Yes, sir," I call loudly after him. He doesn't react. All the kids are still circled like hungry cats around Jade, but the yellow crime scene tape goes way past her in a big loop up to the building. Why? Nothing there but a bunch of books that look like they fell out of the backpack onto the sidewalk, spilling off the curb... It's Jade's backpack, definitely, but are these really Jade's books, or just Mendoza's fake evidence stuff? There's a big book on handguns, a fat math textbook and an even fatter book still in the backpack, barely visible: "Chinese-English Dictionary." I lean down to reach it... I get a sharp cold shiver up my spine. I remember once when I wiped out on my skateboard holding a stack of library books. They scattered just like that. Better leave the books alone, even though no one's watching me. Why'd she drop them? There's no skateboard nearby. The ground's not wet, there's no patch of oil... why did she drop the books? There's one book separate from the others, over by the bike rack. It's scraped, broken open, its spine ripped... a black hair is rising like magic out of the book up into the air, up to the top of the bike rack... it's actually hanging... it's attached to something dark red on the bike rack... with more long black hair hanging...

"Alright, everybody, time's up," snaps Mendoza. "Young man, what'd you find?"

"It's gang related," says Luke, a thick-necked, crew cut boy.

"Evidence?" grumbles Mendoza. "Why was it gang related?"

"Working hypothesis. You find a teen dead, it usually is gangs did it."

"Not wrong, but I didn't ask for a working hypothesis."

"Anyway," pipes up Keeba, "There's no gang clues. No colors. No tattoos. No tags."

Except for Jade's arms. She's got long scars on the inside of both her forearms. You can see the skin is smooth and a lot lighter in certain areas. It looks like she had some tattoos there once. Must have been a bitch to get rid of them. I know, 'cause I had 'Danny' taken off my ankle. Shit, that hurt. And the scar is still there, reminding me of my lamest boyfriend ever.

"She *was* gang," I say. That gets Mendoza's attention. And Jade's: her eyes blink open.

"Don't speak out of turn. You raise your hand if you know the answer. What do you mean?" Mendoza asks slowly.

"But not anymore." I point. "Long scars on the inside of both arms. Where the Asian gangs have their tattoos. Looks like a tatt removal."

Mendoza looks over at Jade, and back at me. He looks super surprised. Jade pulls her sleeves down as far as they'll go.

"That's not true," Keeba sneers. A few others snicker. Some roll their eyes. I can't blame them; they don't want me here and I don't want to be here. I don't owe Keeba anything but maybe I'll help her out with her ignorance problem.

"I know what I'm talking about."

76

"Bull," she spits out. A few others laugh. They're looking for a fight.

Mendoza steps between me and Keeba.

"Okay everybody, let's get back to forensics," he says. "Cooper, that's accurate info about the Asian gangs, but it's not a clue."

"Then it was just an accident," I interrupt while raising my hand. He opens his mouth to yell at me, but stops.

"Why?" He's looking at me now differently like maybe he's actually interested in what I might say.

"The textbook's twisted, the spine's torn and the cover is scraped. It's hard to tear the spine of a hardcover book. Takes a lot of force. But it could happen if someone stepped on the cover and slipped. And while she was slipping, she could have spun around and smashed the back of her head on the corner of the bike rack. There's hair and blood on the corner of the rack."

All the kid-cops look to Mendoza to see if I'm right. He nods in my direction–what's that look? A grudging respect? Anybody laughing now?

"It's not all murder and mayhem," says Mendoza. "Sometimes, detective work confirms an accidental death. Don't assume anything. And look around. Evidence does not line up for your convenience. It lurks where you don't expect it."

The school bell rings.

"Dismissed," Mendoza calls. The cadets break away towards the building.

Jade stands up, stretching stiffly, and wipes the fake blood off her face with her sleeve. As she walks away with the other kids, she turns back to give me a second look—a look laced with something new, like I haven't seen before from her, almost like fear. Like she's afraid of me.

Chapter Sixteen

Thank god school is over. I didn't bring a change of clothes, but luckily my jeans jacket was in my backpack. I throw it on over this hideous uniform and free my dreads. I slam down my skateboard and head down the sidewalk, skating between groups of kids huddling in their little cliques.

Stephan, a geek from cop school, steps in my path with his hand up. He was the courtroom bailiff. He's super tall and very pale. I hop off my board.

"You're out of uniform," he says.

"It's after school. Am I supposed to sleep in this damn thing?"

"You're a cadet first, before anything else."

"Oh, give me a break. It's not a friggin' club."

Stephan Geek actually pulls out a citation pad and begins writing me a ticket.

"I'm citing you for being out of uniform on school grounds."

Jade steps in front of him. He cowers.

"Out of here, Stephan, I got this."

Stephan starts to argue with Jade, but she's got no patience for him. I am sensing she's higher on the totem pole than he is.

She waits till he leaves, then turns to me with ice in her eyes. "How the hell do you know about my tats?"

"I spent time touring with my mom's band. I pick up a thing or two. Lighten up."

"Tourists don't visit with the gangs."

"Yeah, maybe their mother's roadies do if they're looking for supplies. And maybe I was hooking up with one of the roadies. But only on condition he took me wherever he went. Mom's lawyers like me all safe in the hotel room, but I like to see the sights, know what I mean?"

Jade's listening, but she's not totally following my story, because suddenly her attention snaps to a white shiny Range Rover cruising slowly past. The driver is a thin, craggy Asian guy. Jade steps behind me to avoid being seen. When he passes, she tries the icy look again.

"What you bang?" she almost spits. She's not getting it.

"What I what? Don't you mean who do I bang?"

"You know what I mean."

We glare at each other–like I'm gonna take her shit.

"Why would I join a stupid gang?" I ask her.

She backs down, slowly. "You don't run with a gang, do you? I believe it. Only don't bring it up again. You understand?"

"Two threats in two days? This partner thing just gets better and better."

The Range Rover cruises past again, slowly. The driver spots Jade before she sees him.

"Who's the creep in the Rover?" I ask her.

She sees him and tenses.

"You don't want to know. Just walk away."

He's watching her like a cobra.

Jade's tough shell dissolves. She looks like a scared kid, almost panicky. She starts walking away from the Range Rover. I walk with her. She's running now, away from the road, into a landscaped area with high hedges. I'm right behind her.

"Go away," she snarls over her shoulder. We are out of sight of the Rover, so she slows down. "I mean it," she whispers, "you don't want to be seen with me."

We look through the bushes and watch the creep drive off.

"You think he'll come back?" I ask.

"No shit."

"Who is he?"

"Frankie," she snaps. Her tough shell is coming back.

"Who's that?"

"My cousin."

"What does he want with you?"

"He wants to kill me," she says slowly, her arms crossed, squinting into the bright sun.

"Really?"

"It's complicated." We make our way out of the bushes. "You wouldn't understand," she says. "I have a complicated family."

My cell phone blings. I look at my phone. It's a reminder text from Zachary to meet him after school.

"Well, at least you have a family."

"What does that mean? Like you don't?"

"Not really. No."

She doesn't say anything. Neither of us wants to talk about

our families. Or anything else. We kind of just look at each other for a minute before walking away in different directions.

Chapter Seventeen

I find Ping's Place tucked behind the columns with the faces. It smells great and I'm starved. I stop in front of the restaurant. There's an old lady blocking the door, flapping her gums at me.

"Hey there," she smiles, her voice eroded by smoking. "You looking for your dad?"

"Maybe." I wobble on my board. How does she know? "Who are you?"

"I'm Victoria Lee Claire. I own this joint." Her arms are loaded down with bangles that jingle when she moves.

She is a small, cheerful woman, probably in her sixties. She's wearing a vintage Chanel suit, high heels and a tall wig. I can tell it's a wig because when she talks it moves back and forth on her head. And I can tell it's vintage Chanel because I read the New York Times Style Page and last week they had a story on vintage Chanel making a come-back. But how she knows I'm looking for Zachary, I've got no idea.

"You look just like him," she says. "Oh, you are a skinny thing, aren't you?" She circles me now, checking me out like I'm some fashion chick. "You remind me of me when I was your age. I was married before I left high school. Had three more husbands since then. The second was Stanley Fong. Handsome, but what a piece of work."

She lights a cigarette and offers me one. I shake my head no.

"Mr. Fong picked me up at the Playboy Mansion. I was a Bunny back then. One of Hef's girls."

She must be talking about Hugh Hefner... but what's she doing? She's standing with her legs close together and her arm held out like she's holding a tray of drinks. She bends her knees and squats down low. She pretends to offer me a fake drink from her fake tray. I don't fake take it.

"There, the official Bunny Dip. I can still get down, but up–not so easy. Give me a hand." I step off my board and pull her up.

"That's how we served the cocktails."

"Okay."

"Mr. Fong bought me this restaurant and most of the buildings on the block. Oh, he kept me so busy I never had time to cheat. But he did. Ran off with one of the waitresses. Can you believe them apples, Kali? Ha."

"It's Kal. How do you know my name?"

"Your dad talks about you all the time." Yeah, right. I'm getting creeped out right about now. "All the time."

A delivery guy calls out to her in Chinese. He's pushing a dolly with two coolers. He opens one to show crabs on ice. Victoria answers him in perfect Chinese and then turns back to me, "He was planning to call you... he was always *planning* to call you."

She gives me a wink and leads the Chinese delivery guy inside.

I go around the corner, to Zachary's apartment and look up. The front door is painted red. It's old, but the paint is shiny fresh. Last time, in the dark, I hadn't even noticed the color. I climb the stairs.

The door is open so I walk in. Zachary's on the couch watching TV, holding a stuffed white rabbit. Not just any TV; it's a clip of my mom on Entertainment Tonight. Mary Hart cuts in:

"Recording artist Melanee Blu is in Hawaii preparing for her comeback tour. Huge in the Nineties, Melanee is having something of a revival. Entertainment Tonight has just learned that she's also recovering from a pain killer addiction at a secret celebrity rehab resort on the big island. No word if the addiction contributed to the 'wardrobe malfunction' lighting up the blogosphere."

Cut to: Melanee on a beach, her blouse blowing open to reveal bare breasts… covered by a black bar.

"Melanee seemed unaware her top was unbuttoned," says Mary Hart, innocently.

Right. Sure. "Except she rehearsed it with her manager," I blurt out.

If you want to be accurate, Mary, it's Vicodin she's addicted to. And no way she's breaking her habit. That's just something her publicist, Melissa, dreamed up. They fought over how to kick-start publicity for the tour. Her manager, Nigel pushing the open blouse strategy, Melissa convinced that rehab would play better with her older demographic. Typical Melanee that she chose to go with both at once. I guess it's working.

Now they're showing a clip of an old music video:

Coming. She's sporting her traditional heroin-chic look.

I grab the clicker and turn off the TV. Zachary was just reaching for the remote too. Now he's staring at the blank TV.

"Always hated that song. Shows you what I know. Two Grammy's later, she's a sensation." He's still holding the stuffed white rabbit. Now he's stroking its ears, his eyes focused far away. Has he forgotten I'm here?

"What's with the rabbit?" He looks at me like he *did* forget. He gets up, pacing. "What's with any of this stuff?" He motions around the room. "Does it do anything for you? Gross you out? Give you a kick? Is it beautiful?"

"Beautiful?" I look at the crash test dummy in the swing.

"If somebody made it, and it's beautiful, maybe it's art."

"Not according to my art teacher. She says beauty corrupts the truth."

"There's a special circle in hell for her type."

I spot this weird wiggly aluminum statue about six inches high and pull it off the shelf. "What's this, a robot dildo?"

"Well could be. It's a turn of the century French condom mold. And this..." He holds up a hand carved out of wood. "It's a press for making leather gloves. Milan 1880. Found art. I love the fact that these pieces were once part of someone's everyday jobs."

"Why do you have it all shoved into your apartment?"

"I collect it. Sometimes I sell it, deal it."

"I thought you were a limo driver."

"Tough times."

"So what, you don't play music anymore?"

"Not really. I mean sure, I play music, but I don't really *play it.* Is that what you mean?"

I gingerly touch a pair of high-heeled feet sticking out of one end of an ornate box on legs.

"What's this?"

"Saw-The-Lady-In-Half box. This one dates back to 1957. I found it recently in a warehouse in Oxnard." He's walking around the box now and checking it out. "I'm gonna refinish it. Get the patina to come back. Repaint the gold leaf."

"It's pretty big."

He runs his hand along to top. "Yeah, I know, I should really get it out of here."

"It looks like the wicked witch after the house landed on her."

I open the lid and see it's just two wooden feet nailed to the inside.

Zachary protests, "Don't open it. You're not supposed to know the secret."

"And you are?" I pick up a huge saw lying inside the box.

"I'm a magician. I have to know the secret."

"So now you're a magician also?"

"I was when I was a kid. Performed in middle school. Really, don't touch it. Put down the saw." The guy's a nervous wreck, but I don't see why he can't show me the trick. I guess I'll figure it out myself. There's an old cassette tape player inside the box. I take it out and press the play button. Classic magician's music permeates the room with its syrupy twangs. This is so wacked. Zachary's pacing again... is it my problem he needs to relax? I put the tape player on the floor and start to pose to the music–like a real magician's assistant, holding the saw above my head, with a big fake smile.

"Did you ever think about me over these years?" I ask.

That surprises him. He mumbles, "of course." I'm not helping him relax, I know, but this music is inspirational. And the saw gives me superpowers. It's about five feet long, with sharp thin teeth and heavy wooden handle.

"Why didn't you visit me? Where were you anyway?"

"Right here. Can you please put down the saw?" He reaches for it, but I back away.

No way. "In seven years, you never called. Not once." He tries again to grab the saw from me. I scoot around to the other side of the box.

"You never called *me*," he blusters

"I'm the kid," I shout. Why am I wasting my time? He's not going to tell me anything.

"Give me the saw," he insists very seriously.

"Fathers are supposed to care." I hear myself shouting.

"Who are you to judge?" he yells.

"Hello, who am I? I'm your daughter. I guess you forgot. For years!"

"Don't threaten me, don't look at me like that, don't be your mother, don't use that saw, don't do it. Don't do it." He's freaking out.

Suddenly he rushes around the box and grabs at the saw. This guy is nuts. I let him take the saw. Jeez. That seems to help. He backs away. I climb inside the box.

"I was going to call you," he tells me, very quiet now.

"Oh give me a break. After years of hell, then seven years of silence, now suddenly you're a good guy?" I try to squeeze all the way in, but it's so tight.

"I never said I was a good guy," he says, offended.

"Is there a secret panel underneath or something I hide

under?"

"I was going to. I was planning to. It's just that, I mean…" he fades to silence.

Maybe he really was going to call. The old lady downstairs seemed to think so.

"Saw me in half."

"You won't fit.

"When were you going to call? When I was all grown up? Saw me in half."

"You're too tall."

"No, I'm not." I scrunch up into a tight ball. "For Christ's sake, show me how this trick works."

"No."

I'm squirming around so much, trying to fit, that the box almost tips over. Zachary grabs at the box to steady it.

"Don't blame me if you get stuck," he says. "The secret is to fit yourself in this end, this half of the box. Scoot up." I slide away from the fake feet.

"You have to twist a bit, your head here." I lie down and put my neck in some kind of neck brace, facing the ceiling, my whole head outside the end of the box.

"Now curl your legs up even further under you. Sideways." I do what he says. He guides my ankles and elbows to the correct places. He slides in a panel that keeps my legs in my half of the box. It's pretty tight. He then closes the lid over my body and latches the box shut. All of a sudden I am totally trapped. I can't even move my head. Did I really just let him lock me into a box? He's still holding the saw. What if he's some kind of psychopath and he's gonna kill me or something? Does anybody even know where I am? Think, Kal, think... No, don't, don't think about it, Kal, because nobody knows where you are. You could disappear totally. In two pieces.

"We all have a good side and a bad side; my good side is winning," he says slowly, calmly.

"Good side, bad side." I say. "So happy for you. I hope you had lots of fun," Probably not smart, but I'm not thinking too carefully. He holds the huge saw up over his head. He's moving to the music, gesturing along the length of the blade, touching the teeth gingerly, slipping into performance mode. Or maybe he's going mad.

"Ladies and Gentlemen," his voice booms loudly and ominously over the music, "this saw is made of hardened steel, steel that can slice through bone," here he flaps the saw violently so it twangs loudly, "Through bone, I say, and sever sinews faster than you can draw breath to scream." He's slipping the saw into the slot in the middle of the box. He's sawing downwards. "Faster than thought..."

"Can we do it without the spiel?" I interrupt.

He seems agitated. He lets go of the saw, which falls right through the slot, hits the bottom of the box, tips down where the heavy handle hangs outside the box, twangs loudly for a moment and then flops down and crashes to the floor. "I was so anxious about calling you, so anxious. Very stressful."

I have got to stop upsetting him. But before I can think of what to say, he continues.

"Don't you have any clue?" He's sputtering. "Any clue how much I love you? All of this new life, the rehab, the sobriety..."

I'm not buying it. "Yeah, right. You're a total drunk." I

must be suicidal, but he's totally bugging me.

"You know nothing about me," he growls. "Nothing!" I have to look far to the right, straining my neck, to even see him. He's standing stock still, red in the face.

I suddenly really want to get out of the box.

"Let me out. Zachary." But he is not listening to me.

"And it was all for you," he says, coming closer. "To prove to you I could do it. But I assumed you hated me and I hated myself even more, and so I was waiting till the time was right…"

"Let me out." I'm trying to move, bit by bit getting the box to rock back and forth. Zachary grabs at it, steadies it and undoes the latch. I try to leap just out as Zachary pulls out the divider, which trips me, and I start to fall… Zachary catches me, sort of, falling backwards himself as I grab the box instead, which tips over, crashing loudly almost of top of both of us as we tumble to the floor in a heap. Neither of us moves for a few seconds. The magician's music plays on, it's perky, fast guitar still trying to hide the deep sadness in the old gypsy melody.

"Don't hate me, Kali."

"Hate you? I don't hate you. But I hate this music." I reach over to the tape player and hit the stop button.

"None of that's true," he says as I try to disentangle myself from Zachary and the box. "You do hate me, but, it's okay. I hate myself. And you loved gypsy music when you were little. You don't outgrow that shit."

Chapter Eighteen

The phone rings. Zachary's got some kind of old-fashioned phone that plugs into the wall and the handle is attached to the phone by a cord. It even has a round dial with numbers.

"Aren't you going to get that?" I ask. But he stays lying on the ground and lets it ring. I mean, he tries to get up, but the box is on his legs. I should help him, but I'm lying on the giant saw so I better move slowly. There's a tear in my pants above the knee. Skin is scraped, but not bad.

The answering machine picks up and a kid's voice is on the other end. The voice is faint but clear.

"Zachary, I, ummmmm, I got arrested. I'm downtown at the Central Community Police Station. It's Marley."

That gets his attention. I help him lift the box off his legs. No major harm done, it seems as he scurries up but he's in some pain. "Awwww."

When he gets to the phone, she's already hung up. He's totally bummed that he missed her call and slumps down in his desk chair rubbing his legs.

"What was that about?"

"That's Marley. I'm her CASA."

Zachary picks up the phone. He dials 411.

"Her what?"

"C-A-S-A. CASA is an acronym for Court Appointed Special Advocate. Marley's a foster kid. When all the grownups are battling it out in court, I make sure someone is looking out for her."

"How old is she?"

"Twelve."

Someone on the other end of the phone must be talking 'cause he says, "Los Angeles. Central Community Police Station." He writes something down on a piece of paper and then grabs his keys and cell phone off the desk.

"Come on, Kal. We gotta go." He plugs a number into his cell.

"Where? And why do I have to go?"

He points to the clock. It's almost six o'clock.

"Curfew. Let's go." He limps toward the door.

"Sure, anything for Marko."

"Marley."

"Whatever."

He's standing there holding the door open for me and I suddenly get this really weird flashback to when I was little. I remember him standing in that same spot, holding that same red door. Him saying, "Let's go." But I don't think I was ever in this room before. I mean, before I broke into it the other day. In my flashback I don't want to go with him.

"You okay?" he says, but his voice sounds far away. Anyway, I'm busy, I'm thinking: Am I hearing this right? Is he really spending time making sure some other kid is being taken care of after their parents have bailed on them?

He's reaching for my hand. I guess he's trying to get me to move. My hands go in my pockets and I turn my back on him. The room is stuffed with so many lifeless statues and dolls and mannequins. I want to talk to them, ask them what they've seen the last few years, find out what my dad was doing, what he's doing now, what he's thinking now, what he's doing rushing off to help some total stranger when here I am, his daughter, in his face. He's ignored me my whole life. Okay, so maybe I wasn't arrested when I was twelve, or in prison, but living with Melanee is its own kind of prison… as you know damn well yourself… at least you got away, you selfish piece of…

"Yeah, yeah, I'm fine." I follow him out and he locks the door behind me.

Chapter Nineteen

We're at the Central Community Police Station in Downtown Los Angeles. It's your typical cop shop. And just like it looks on TV, nothing like the cement bunker by the sea. This is a big room with rows of cubicles with lots of desks and cops sitting at them. Xerox's of wanted people taped to the walls. Folding chairs line one wall, me on one of them. I'm drooling onto my thumb, trying to get some saliva onto the scrape on my leg, but it's mostly ending up on my pants.

A cop, a young African American, wants my attention. She leads me to a small room with a glass wall, a desk and a long beat-up wooden bench. There's a lot of waiting in police stations, I've decided. Then after a while some chick shuffles in. She's wearing a pink velvety running suit with a tight yellow tee-shirt underneath that shows off her killer bod. She's super tall and kind of awkward. She's wearing a baseball cap turned sideways. She gives me a little thin smile. Zachary comes in behind her.

"Marley, this is Kali, Kal, she's my daughter," he says.

Which is very weird to hear, him calling me his daughter.

And pretty weird to think this girl is twelve. She looks at least seventeen.

Marley takes off her baseball cap and plays with her blonde hair. The right side is cut short above her ear and the left side is below her chin.

"I got it cut at Floyd's 99 Barbershop just like Rihanna's," she says to me. "I drew them a picture of how I wanted it. I look just like her, right?"

"Yeah, you do," if Rihanna were a twelve year old white girl.

She studies my hair very closely. "I like your dreads. I'm gonna do that next." She holds out her hand towards my hair. "Can I touch them?"

Zachary pulls Marley down on to the bench before she reaches my hair. He's trying to get the story of how she got arrested and she's trying not to tell him much. She's not really listening to him, but looking sideways at me standing in the doorway. Her eyes are squinting... fair enough, there's a big window behind me, but her squint is more like she's interested in me. I haven't had someone look at me that intensely since... I don't think it's ever happened. The squint also makes tiny lines around her eyes, making her look even older. Zachary is frustrated he can't get her attention. Maybe I should get out of the way.

"Bathroom," I say, and go off to find it. The bathroom's pretty decent, so I take my time, wash my face and clean off my cut.

When I get back Marley is whispering to Zachary.

"It's better than what I've got. At least I'd be safe."

Zachary shakes his head "Really and truly, jail isn't the

safe place you're looking for, Marley."

Just then this fat lady bursts past me, knocking me out of the doorway.

"Marley!" she calls out all loud and gushy.

Turns out she's Roseanne Parker, Marley's foster mother. Roseanne is big city trailer trash: tasteless but tidy, uptight yet flabby, bulging out of a sixty-dollar retro t-shirt of Cookie Monster holding a rhinestone-studded chocolate chip cookie.

"Hey, watch it." I tell her. But she could care less about me. She's got her eye on Marley, who cowers close to Zachary.

"I don't want to go home with her. Don't make me, Zachary."

Roseanne throws her fake Louis Vuitton bag down on the bench.

"See what you went and did?" Roseanne whines at Zachary. "Now you got her all up and against me. Like you're on her side."

"I'm *supposed* to be on her side," says Zachary. "Which is the same side you're supposed to be on." All right, Zachary.

"You've got no right to corrupt her against me."

"If you mean…"

"Don't get smart on me. You know what I mean. Enjoy your power while you've got it, because I've got news for you which is I'm going to adopt her, so then you'll have to butt the hell out."

Marley stares at Zachary, her voice is tiny, desperate: "Can't I go home with you?"

"Sorry, kiddo. You know you can't. You need to go home with Roseanne. She's your legal guardian. But you can always call me."

"There's nothing you can do?" she almost cries as she jumps up. "Please, please, there's nothing?" Her knees are wobbling.

Nobody moves... except Zachary, who gets up slowly. He looks over at Roseanne, then at me. He's holding a lot in. Then, sounding calm, he says to Marley, "Be strong."

Roseanne pops little noises out of her mouth, like she wants to say something but her brain can't keep up. Her tiny eyes glare. A cop slips past me into the room.

"You her guardian?" The cop holds a clipboard out to Zachary.

Roseanne grabs the clipboard from the cop. "That's for me. You think he's her guardian? Him?" She snorts. "I'm her guardian. Ain't that right, Marley?"

"Yes, ma'am," Marley whimpers. She seems so scared of Roseanne.

I never realized before how much the word guardian sounds like guard. Could be like a lifeguard who saves you, a security guard who protects you or a prison guard who slams you down. Roseanne is Marley's prison guard for sure.

The police officer takes the clipboard from Roseanne and hands it to Marley to sign. "You are free to go home now with your foster mom," the officer says. "Stay out of trouble. Got it? Now I need a word with the adults here a moment."

The cop pulls Zachary and Roseanne outside the room and talks to them quietly so me and Marley can't hear. Marley rips a corner off a magazine she's been holding and scribbles something on it. She keeps glancing at me.

The cop comes back in. "We're done here." He hands

Zachary and Roseanne his card. "Call me if you need to discuss anything."

I step outside the office as the cop leads Marley, Roseanne and Zachary out the front doors of the cop station. We all walk outside. As Marley passes me, she slips the torn-off piece of magazine into my hand. Then she leans back on her heels and skates on two wheels that come out of the soles of her shoes. "Wheelies," she calls back to me.

"Drug possession?" Roseanne sneers at Marley. "How stupid could you be?" She hits Marley on the side of the head, but Marley sees it coming and dodges enough that the blow glances off. The officer, busy with some papers, doesn't see it.

"Hey!" Furious, I lunge at Roseanne. Zachary steps in my way, blocks me. He shakes his head. Roseanne and Marley go off to the parking structure. The cop goes back inside.

"How can you do that?" I ask Zachary. "How can you just let her go off with that nasty fat-ass?"

Why doesn't he *do* anything?

We watch as Marley skates towards Roseanne's car.

"What was the cop talking to you and Roseanne about?"

"Marley's been in trouble a lot. If she's arrested again, she's going to jail. He wanted us to understand that." He turns and walks on. I stay back and read the paper Marley gave me: there's an address on Dudley Avenue. Then it says, Attic, Friday, 9:00 P.M., Venice. Plez come.

Zachary calls back, "What you got there?"

"Nothing." I crumble up the paper and stick it in my jeans pocket.

"You coming?"

"Yeah," I run and catch up with him. I know I should tell

him. But Marley didn't give him the address, she gave it to me. And it's an attic, at night. I'm thinking Zachary would say something doesn't sound right.

Chapter Twenty

Zachary pulls the limo up to the drive-thru speaker at In-n-Out Burger and we listen to some burn-out burger boy mumble a phony welcome through a crappy speaker.

"What do you want?" Zachary asks me.

Honestly? I want an answer. "You were saving all these other kids and you left me with my screwed up mom all these years?"

Zachary flinches a bit. I meant that to hurt so that's good.

"What do you want to eat?"

"Why don't you answer my question?"

"It wasn't a question. It was an attack."

The crappy speaker is saying something; probably somebody inside wants us to order.

"Double double animal style and fries." I yell at the speaker. That's a double burger with grilled onions and extra spread. For himself he orders a 3x3, three burgers, three pieces of cheese.

"For me, it's about the quantity," he tells me.

"Mom went vegan last year."

"Seriously? The whole thing? Like nothing animal at all?"

"Not even honey."

"Honey?" He can't believe it. "Why honey?"

"Nothing with eyes."

"Well, at least she can't eat you," says Zachary, almost chuckling as he drives to the pick-up window. He feels around in his pockets.

"Shit I didn't grab my wallet." He opens the glove compartment and fumbles around for some loose change.

"Here, I'll get it." I pull my credit card out of my pocket, reach over him and hand it to the cashier in the window. Zachary tries to hand me the loose change he's gathered. Like I want a pocket full of dirty money. He looks hurt. I guess I was rolling my eyes and sneering like my mom always says I do.

We drive to the next window and wait for our food. I fumble with the radio stations. He pushes the off button. It's really quiet in the car. He looks like he's trying to avoid looking at me, but maybe I'm making that up. Maybe his mind is just far away. Then he just starts talking.

"I got arrested a couple years back," he says quietly. "DUI. I got community service. So, while I was cleaning trash off the side of the highway feeling sorry for myself, I met this kid who was in foster care. He told me about his life. My life suddenly seemed really good compared."

"Your order's ready." He takes the bag of food from the burger kid in the window and drives around the back to the parking area.

"After a couple of months, I kept thinking about this kid and his rotten, shitty life. I didn't know how to find him. I never did find him but I found this program. Marley is the fourth kid I've been a CASA to."

He pulls the limo into a parking space and hands me the bag of burgers. I'm trying to be nice, but.

"Isn't it a little weird that you helped these kids and never called me?" I know I'm repeating myself, but I still want to know and he's not telling.

A strong street lamp shines straight down on us, spotlighting the bright white paper and colors of the burger packaging on my lap. It takes him a long time to answer, and then he doesn't actually answer.

"It's a long story."

As I open my burger I get a text from Dakota. We text back and forth while I eat my burger. Zachary checks his email on his phone; he's fine, he doesn't want to talk any more than I do. Dakota wants me to stay over tonight. I'm not sure how to tell Zachary…

"I don't know what I'm gonna do with you tonight," says Zachary. "I work nights. That's when I take the limo out. Gotta meet someone at LAX in an hour." Sometimes things just work out.

"You can take me over to my friend's house. I can stay there."

"I can't leave you without an adult."

"My friend's mom is home."

He looks at me like I'm lying, which I am.

"Well, okay. Just till I figure this out. Maybe I can change my shift to days."

He starts the car and I give him directions to Dakota's house. Then I text Dakota, telling him I'm on my way.

We drive up Lincoln Boulevard towards Santa Monica. He

takes a left on Ocean Park, up over the hill where you can start to see the ocean. Then a right on Pacific and left onto Fraser Avenue.

"I've been here before." He points up to a condo across the street. "Margaux Hemmingway lived there. Killed herself in that house. "

"Who's Margaux Hemmingway?"

"A model, actress. She's Mariel Hemmingway's sister, you know, star of the movie, *Manhattan*."

"I never saw it."

He looks at me like I'm from Mars.

"You never saw *Manhattan*? Only one of the greatest movies. Ever see any Woody Allen movies?"

"No."

He starts to parallel park but when he puts the car in reverse I throw open the door. "You don't need to park. I'll get out here."

"Wait, I should meet your friend's mom."

"She's asleep. She goes to bed early 'cause she has to be on a movie set first thing in the morning." Not entirely a lie. She probably is asleep and most likely has to be on set early. He doesn't need to know she's in Boston.

"You gonna be able to get to school on time from here?"

"Yes."

"How about I pick you up after school? We'll go get burgers again."

"No, thanks."

I slam the door shut. He rolls down the window and calls out, "I'll see you after school tomorrow."

I start walking and try to tune him out of my brain. I look

up at Dakota's house. He's watching from his bedroom window. I beat it inside and up to Dakota's room. I join him at the window.

We watch as Zachary tries to turn the limo around on the narrow street. "That him?" Dakota asks.

"Yeah. He told me some chick killed herself in the house across the street."

"Not just some chick, Margaux Hemmingway. Granddaughter of Earnest Hemmingway, sister to Mariel who was in the greatest freaking movie of all time."

Oh, great. They both love the same greatest freaking movie of all time. We watch Zachary back into a driveway and finally make the three-point turn.

"I don't think he knows he's on a one way street," Dakota says.

"Nope. He's got no idea."

Chapter Twenty-one

We're paired up with our partners today in forensics class, all wearing white lab coats, plastic goggles and rubber gloves. The science lab has tall tables with burners and sinks in them. Each pair has their own table. One wall has giant murals of anime type characters dressed as police officers.

We have to add white powder to test tubes and then pour in vinegar and water. Jade's in charge of our experiment. She barely lets me touch anything.

"What's your problem?" I ask.

She gives me a dead look through the scratched plastic goggles and doesn't answer.

"Okay, I can be a bitch too." I turn away from her and raise my hand.

That gets her attention. "What do you think you're doing?"

"I was just gonna tell Mendoza I'm bored, 'cause my partner won't let me do any of the cool crap."

"Don't." She shoves a beaker at me.

I take it and measure a tablespoon of baking soda. I pour the baking soda into the beaker.

"So where'd you live in Minneapolis?" I ask.

She really doesn't want to talk to me.

"My mom's band played Cabooze on West Bank."

Jade opens up a jar of white vinegar and hands it to me. I smell it: it stinks–like vinegar. "Man, did you ever drink this shit? Nasty."

She's ignoring me.

Mendoza circles us like a mosquito buzzing and hovering. Waiting to land and bite.

"What's happening over here?" he asks. "Is Jade filling you in on how things are done?"

"Yeah, I'm all set."

"Good." Mendoza walks away and I fake smile at Jade. As soon as he's gone I reach in my backpack and take out a piece of gum and stick in my mouth.

Jade glares at me and points to a chart on the wall. It reads:

NO Headsets of any kind on campus.
NO Smoking on campus.
NO Chewing gum on campus.

I take the gum out of my mouth and stick it on her beaker. Suddenly angry, she pulls it off and squashes it onto my beaker.

"I wonder what happens to gum in a solution of vinegar and baking soda?" I say as I drop the gum into my beaker. Nothing happens. Except with Jade, who thinks it's funny. I mean I know she's laughing *at* me, but that's better than her dead glare. Anyway, that lasts two seconds and then it's back to the glare. Maybe we should talk about something else.

"Did it hurt when you got those tats removed?"

Ooh, she didn't like that question. Okay, I am done with the small talk. Usually I can talk with a brick wall, but this chick has some serious 'tude. Five months and twenty-seven days to go. How am I going to put up with this for that long? I can't do it. Mendoza is watching me. Look busy. What am I supposed to be doing? Chemistry, that's right. Maybe I'll become a scientist. That would surprise them all. But it will take time. For now, I better not get kicked out of class.

I open the science book and start reading about the experiment. *Some chemical substances have acidic properties, others, basic properties. Acids are substances which free hydrogen ions (H^+) when they are mixed with water.*

"They put a topical crème on your skin which dulls the pain," says Jade. "That, and I drank like three tallboys." I look up from my book.

She spoke. I nod. Not a fake nod.

"Do you want to type our notes into the computer or do you want me to?" she asks.

"Um, I can. Sure."

"You gotta sign out a laptop. Over there in that cabinet." She points to a gray metal cabinet. "Just sign your name, and the time. Make sure you get a power cord too."

"Okey dokey." I hop off my lab stool and think to myself, *five months and twenty-seven days to go,* maybe I can make it.

The filing cabinet's open and I pull out an outdated PC and a power cord. Next to the laptops is another cabinet that's half open. I look inside. It's full of iPods and small ear pods. They're hanging out of a box labeled Surveillance. There's also another box with a bunch of tiny cameras. I pick up one of the cameras and look through it. Just then, Stephan Geek comes up behind me and slams the cabinet door shut.

"Shit," I spin around. "You almost broke my friggin' finger."

"Stay away from the surveillance stuff. Check out your laptop and go back to your seat."

"Who made you Queen of the country?"

"I'm in charge of the equipment. Did you sign out your laptop yet, or are you planning on lifting it?"

He's such an idiot. I yank the pen from his greasy hand and sign my name on the god damn cabinet door.

I walk back to my station mumbling, "Five months and twenty-seven days, five months and twenty-seven days."

Chapter Twenty-two

The last bell of the day. How hard would it be to make a bell that doesn't sound raspy and awful? I bolt out of my English class towards the lockers. That's when I see Penn - my lawyer in training. But check him out: He's sporting some serious Rude Boy look. Sharkskin suit, fedora hat and skinny tie. He even found himself some pointy-toe black boots. Mr. Dull is looking sharp. I walk up behind him and poke him in the ribs. He spins around and we're standing eye to eye. He looks me over. I imagine he'll make fun of my cop uniform but instead he starts harassing me about my hair.

"How come you gotta rat your hair in dreads? That's not a practical hair style for a white girl."

He's right. It took me eight hours for my mom's stylist to twist my hair into dreads and then wrap them in yarn–definite commitment on my part. So who cares what he thinks.

"You must have spent a ton of your mama's dough on that too. Fake eye color, fake hair." He shakes his head at me.

"How come you don't like anything about me?"

All the cool pose goes sideways and he mumbles some lame, "I didn't mean it like that." I forget sometimes how guys have a hard time with bitchy talk, even though he started it, so I cut him some slack and play with the beads I wove into my dreads last night.

"The sharkskin, the pointy toes, not bad." I spin the wheels of my skateboard that I'm holding in front of me.

He turns towards his locker and pulls out a black and white checkerboard sticker that says–Beat Boyz. He peels the backing off and sticks it to the bottom of my skateboard.

"You're in a Ska band?" I start laughing.

"What's so funny about that?"

"Nothing, you just, I don't know, you didn't seem the type to play music."

"And you are some sort of expert about music people I assume because your mom is a rock legend?"

Now he's more flustered and starts to rip the sticker off my board. I don't let him and put my board around behind me. I hate that he brought up my mom.

"Anyway, you're right," he tells me under his breath. "I represent the Beat Boyz. I manage them. I don't play with them,"

He turns back to his locker and shoves some books into a US Postal mail-bag–nice touch.

"I know this girl," I tell him. "She needs to get into your program."

"She need a lawyer?"

"She needs to get into Teen Court. Her name's Marley."

"We're full up with clients for the semester. It's a popular program."

"You gotta do better than that."

"Get me her 4-1-1. I'll talk to the judge. No promises."

"Didn't you promise to get me out of cop school?"

He slams his locker and looks at me. "Still working on it." He turns to walk down the hall and here I go following him again.

"I'm gonna die there."

"Spare me the details," he says, looking me up and down without looking like he is. "You don't look like you're dying."

He turns a corner and we go down another hall. "You see the sketches of us?"

"What sketches?"

Penn stops outside of the art room. Then I see them. A bunch of courtroom charcoal drawings from Teen Court taped to the wall. Penn stops in front of one. It's me slumped in a chair looking humiliated and him standing–pointing at the judge.

"I think he nailed your essence," says Penn.

"I look like a criminal."

"You are a criminal."

"Great. You defend the artist, but you can't defend me."

"Just how much attention do you need, girl?"

"Screw you." Okay, so that was pathetic. But that hurt and I always sound stupid when I'm hurt. How much do I need? I don't think I need any, I sure don't want any, but everybody all my life keeps saying I act like I want it. Attention. Screw them all. How about if I just disappear? What'll they say then: 'Oh good, I guess she doesn't need attention any more?'

Penn is looking at me a little sorry, like he's going to apologize. Thank god his cell phone rings. He checks caller ID. "My new client, busted for shoplifting. Catch you later." He answers the phone and wanders down the hall, talking, but he spins around twice, his eyes locking with mine each time. Why the hell am I letting that happen?

Have to remember he's a dork, a lawyer. Everything I hate. It's the suit, that's what I'm looking at. And the boots. You can't blame me… they're good boots.

I head down the hallway on the way out. I feel my phone in my pocket vibrate. I pull out the phone and see it's a text from Zachary. It says: WAITING OUTSIDE OF SCHOOL 4U.

Kind of the last thing I want to do right now is hang with Zachary. I'm gonna skateboard back to Dakota's instead. He's making a dress for me out of his old tee-shirts. I put on my Bluetooth headset and pocket my phone. No texting for a while.

I walk towards the side door so I can slip out without Zachary seeing me. That's when I see a guy holding Jade's hand, at the end of Main Hall. He's about twenty-four, Asian-American, the same guy I saw in the white SUV. Jade's cousin, Frankie. He's wearing a Laker's jersey with a metal chain around his neck. His sneakers are bright white. I watch as he and Jade barrel down the hall towards me. But something's wrong: Frankie holds Jade's hand too hard, too twisted.

I call out to her, "Jade, you cool?"

She tries to smile, but I know it's fake, "Yeah, I'm cool."

I give them some distance and then follow them to the front door.

As soon as we're outside I see Zachary's giant stretch black limo hanging out in the school drop-off zone. Jesus, how could he not think that would be incredibly embarrassing? Like I need these kids watching me get into a limo. Then I see

Zachary; he's standing on the big lawn outside the school. He's looking for me. Oh, man. I gotta keep my eye on Jade, so I do my best to avoid Zachary–which is not easy since he's got a pretty good view. He waves me over to the car and heads back to his limo without looking back, probably thinking I'm following him. But I'm on Jade.

Frankie walks Jade over to his white Range Rover. It's parked half a block in front of the limo. He opens the passenger door, but Jade suddenly decides she's not getting in. She kicks at Frankie, spinning as she does, trying to get her hand out of his grip. It doesn't work. It looks like she's in agony, but she doesn't scream. Why doesn't she scream? She must know that will just make things worse. Frankie wraps his other hand around the back of her neck and shoves her head first into the car, slamming the door behind her. He runs around to the driver's seat and starts the car. Jade looks out the window–clearly scared–and catches my eye. I slip behind the Rover, crouched low.

"Kal!" Zachary's calling me, but I'm busy now. I throw down my skateboard and grab the underside of the rear bumper of the Rover. I'm low and to the right, so the driver can't see me. The Rover takes off, the right rear tire kicking up gravel to sting my knees. That's better; I can handle this. Just me and my board and I'm in control. I'm good at skitching.

Chapter Twenty-three

I hang on tight as the Range Rover barrels down Venice Boulevard toward the beach. Frankie's running yellows and flooring it like gas was made to be guzzled. Luckily the road is pretty new, so I'm riding smooth, but you never know what crap is coming at you, so I lean out to the right to check the road. Dangerous of course, since Frankie could see me in his rearview, but I'm quickly back behind and that's the chances you got to take. Now some asshole in a convertible is honking, pointing at me, trying to get Frankie's attention. Frankie speeds up. The guy drops away.

My phone rings. I push my Bluetooth to answer. It's Zachary shouting, "What the hell are you doing?"

"I'm kinda busy right now."

"I'm right behind you."

I look back and sure enough the limo is closing in.

"I'm Rover-surfing, what does it look like?"

"Get the hell off the car–now! Let go, Kali."

Frankie makes a fast lane change to the right. I almost lose my grip on the tight swerve. The limo stays close. Zachary's still yelling at me.

"Hold on. No, let go, let go!"

I'm fine, but the limo is too close, like a killer whale on my ass. If I have to release, I'll need space. "Back off. Don't let him see you." Then wouldn't you know it, of all times, I get call waiting.

"Wait, hold on a sec. Call waiting." I switch calls and say, "Hello?"

Then I hear that smooth, slinky voice that sold five million records, Melanee Blu, AKA: Total Loser Mom.

For a moment I have to concentrate as we cross Lincoln Boulevard. It's kinda rough. I could sure use some bigger wheels about now.

She's blabbing away, "We finally got the vocal tracks right, then this shitty drummer that's filling in for Benny says to me..."

I interrupt, "Mom, this is a really bad time."

"Oh, I see. A bad time. Well, it usually is with you..."

"Mom, I'm skitching a Range Rover on Venice and Zachary is chasing us..."

"Zachary? Save it, Kali It's not funny. Not in the mood. I called to get a little sympathy from you and–"

"And I don't have time for you right now." I hang up on her and switch back to Zachary. Kind of odd for me, never happened before: both parents on the phone at the same time, but Venice Boulevard west of Lincoln is old and I'm one pothole from dead.

"Zachary, I gotta go."

"You could get yourself killed."

"Stop acting like you care."

The Rover switches to the left lane.

"Look out!" Zachary shouts.

There's more traffic. Zachary, trying to stay behind the Rover, cuts in front of another car. The big limo doesn't cut well; it wobbles and tires screech. More honking.

"I'm sorry I never called you all these years, Kal."

"Focus, Dad."

The limo is way too close again.

"I thought you hated me."

"I do," I say.

"You called me 'Dad'."

The Rover brakes hard and turns left suddenly. I barely hang on. Where's he going? South on Dell? That goes through the canals. Oh, I get it. He's seen the limo and Dell is the perfect street to lose a limo: it goes over the canals on tiny, narrow bridges with huge high humps. Oh god. It's a great place to destroy a skitcher, too. The canals are one of the few things left from the original Venice created by Abbot Kinney a hundred years ago; it's now a tight neighborhood of fancy houses with narrow walkways between the houses and the canals. There's only one road that goes through the neighborhood, Dell, and it's a roller coaster of four small hump-backed bridges.

Zachary follows. Relentless. Do either of these idiots know what they are doing? Up over the first bridge, shit, the Rover goes airborne over the top... I can't hold on, so now I'm surfing down the backside of the bridge, making fast sharp turns and scraping my tail to slow down. The Rover is bouncing badly, fishtailing, almost hitting the cars parked along the sides of the houses; he's losing control, the top-heavy tub teetering back and forth as he over-corrects, guns the engine, one wheel biting asphalt and the other spinning on dirt, then even the wheel on asphalt starts spinning, burning rubber into a white cloud that mixes with the dust from the dirt to almost hide the big boat as it drifts in slow motion into a construction dumpster. Seemed like slow motion but it must have been fast, because the airbags go off and the driver's door is smashed in.

I stop behind the Rover. I kick up my board, grab it, and glance back at the bridge. It's ugly: the limo's nose shoots up over the hump of the bridge, drops over the top, crunching hard, scraping metal along the whole long underside, screeching and sending sparks from under the car like it's exploding. Which it will, if the gas tank breaks. But the big whale is strong and it's got just enough momentum to drag its long shiny black ass over the bridge.

A door slams. Jade is jumping out the other side of the Rover, running to me. Frankie tries to open the driver's side door, but it's jammed.

Jade yells at me. "What the hell are you doing?"

"I thought you needed help," I say, leading her quickly to the limo.

"You're crazy, girl."

"Get in the limo!" I open the back door. Jade looks through the windshield at Zachary.

"Who's this?"

"Temporary Custody," I say. "Get in."

She doesn't want to. She does want to. She doesn't. She looks back at Frankie, who's climbing out the passenger side door.

Jade is desperate: she looks me in the eye, really looks at

me, trying, I think, to decide if she can she trust me. Maybe she decides she doesn't have much of a choice and dives in the limo headfirst. I slide in after her, stumbling and rolling on the floor. Jade clambers onto a seat and peers out the closed window. Frankie hobbles up to the limo, clutching his side. He must have gotten hurt in the crash. He bangs his fist on our door, trying to pull it open.

"He's going to kill us," yells Jade.

I guess Zachary believes her. He guns the limo in reverse. Frankie stumbles after us, twisted sideways in pain. I gotta hand it to Zachary, he can sure drive. He blasts the whale back over the bridge, backwards. It's a very narrow bridge. The hump tears at the underside again, freaky loud, but we make it over. Half way down the block is an alley with just enough room to turn a limo around in. Zachary makes the turn quickly and heads back to Venice Boulevard. No sign of Frankie. Maybe the Range Rover was too damaged to drive.

Zachary slides open the partition between the front and back seat and asks, "You okay?"

"Yeah," we both say at the same time.

"Who's your friend, Kal?"

"I'm Jade. We're not friends, we're just in the same class."

"Who's that guy?"

"My cousin Frankie. He's with a gang."

"And what's he want with you?"

"He wants me to be his mule."

Now I get it. Mules transport drugs inside their bodies. I feel sick.

"I'm serious," Zachary says.

Jade's voice is icy cold: "They killed my brother. Frankie's one of the leaders."

Zachary takes a deep breath. "Great, really great, so I crashed a big gangster's car. I'm assuming he's not going to like that, is he?"

"I tried to not get in the car," says Jade. "Anyway, you shouldn't have followed me."

"I got no quarrel with you, Jade," says Zachary. "It's Kal got me into this."

We drive a bit, everybody silent. I could point out that he shouldn't have followed me, but I know why he did. So we don't have to talk about it.

Then Jade says, "I would never be Frankie's mule. He would have had to kill me."

"That's not a very good option," says Zachary.

Jade makes her way to the front of the passenger cabin and looks through the little partition window.

"Thank you," she tells Zachary.

"You're welcome."

Jade clambers back to me. We slide low into our seats. I look over at Jade and see a faint smile on her face.

"You're messed up, Kal."

Chapter Twenty-four

Where do you live?" Zachary's voice crackles from the speaker.

"Olympic Boulevard, off First, can you hear me? Where's the microphone?" Jade is looking around for it.

The speaker again: "I can hear everything you say. So don't talk about me. And stay out of the mini-bar."

"You live downtown?" I ask Jade. "How do you get to school?"

"Bus."

I can't even imagine that–taking a bus ride that long to school.

"Every day? How can you stand it? What is it, like an hour?"

"Yeah, each way." And her eyes add: I don't care what you think.

Zachary drives up Venice Boulevard. I guess he's taking her all the way home. I pry off my sneakers with my toes and flop back on the curvy seat, which slides me way forward on the slippery leather. I'm staring up at the mirror on the ceiling. Jade looks around, touching everything, like she's never been in a limo before. Now I'm curious: why would anybody want to go on a bus two hours a day to learn how to be a cop?

"You must really like cop school."

Jade is suddenly fascinated by the mini-bar. She is not getting into this conversation.

I reach out with my right toe and turn on the lights, all of them hidden and indirect. I hit another button and blackout shades lower over the windows. Red, purple and blue tiny shiny beads, embedded in the ceiling mirrors, pop on. I hit another button with my left toe and the lights begin to flash in different patterns, dancing around the cabin.

Jade gazes at the lights, amazed. Then everything goes sideways: I slip and end up on the floor and Jade does practically a summersault and lands on her back. Zachary is turning the big whale onto a freeway on-ramp. As soon as we straighten out Jade is up and opening some little doors: she finds prepared salads, sushi rolls, potato chips, beer, wine and soft drinks. She pulls out a soda.

"Can I have one of these?" she asks.

Zachary pipes up through the speaker, "No." He slides open the partition window and passes us back two Red Bulls. I take them. They aren't cold, but even a nasty warm Red Bull sounds good right now.

Jade plays with some knobs. "What's this?"

"Sound system." She's really never been in a limo.

"And this one?"

"DVD player."

"Cool." She turns it on. A screen lowers down at the front. It's huge, the width of the whole cabin. A movie begins. Some naked dude is floating in a pool... but then the picture goes blank.

Zachary yells through the little window, "Don't touch the DVD. You can listen to music, but leave everything else alone."

Jade's found an iPod jack. She's pointing at it like it's a prize.

I dread this because there is no way she and I have the same taste in music.

I sit up and start digging for my iPod in my backpack but Jade has beaten me to it. She pulls her iPod from her pocket and plugs it into the jack.

"Lost in America" by Pepper starts playing. Don't tell me she's got decent taste in music? She's looking at me, challenging me. But I lose nothing by liking Pepper too. I don't have to say it.

Jade lies back and pulls off her boots. We watch the tiny colored lights bounce to the beat of the music, drink our warm Red Bulls and float down the freeway like we're on a magic carpet.

Chapter Twenty-five

Zachary pulls off the freeway and I raise a toe to push the button that raises the curtains on the windows. We're in a neighborhood of run-down one-story houses. The limo is getting some attention: people standing on street corners stop their conversations to point. At a stop sign a group of teenagers surround the limo and try to look in the windows at us. Jade curls into a ball to hide.

"They can't see inside," I tell her.

"Can you just get out of here?" she whimpers. "Turn right at the next street."

Zachary turns the corner quickly. Some of the kids try to chase us. Zachary floors it down the next block. Jade looks up to guide him through two more turns.

"That's it," she says.

It's a little house, Spanish style, kinda cute, though the front lawn is patchy crabgrass and the windows are barred.

Jade grabs her boots, throws open the door and runs to the house. She lets herself in. She didn't even say goodbye. I notice she left her iPod so I pull it out of the jack, making it suddenly quiet inside the limo. I start to get out of the limo to take it to her.

"Kal, get up in the front seat," Zachary calls back to me. He sounds kind of pissed. "Now," he yells. As I take the long walk from the back door to the front I see a couple of teens converging on the limo from both ends of the street. They're mostly all dressed in drooping jeans and white T-shirts with tattoos crawling out the top of their shirts and up their necks. I jump in the limo, which is in motion before I close the door.

"She forgot her iPod," I explain.

He's angry. "Gangs now?" he snaps.

"No."

"Bull."

"Jade's not in a gang. She used to be."

"Drugs too?"

"She wants to be a cop."

"But you don't?"

"Look, I don't do drugs, if that's what you're trying to say. That's mom's thing."

"Addictive personalities run in families."

Everybody assumes I'm a druggy because of my mom. Like I'm constantly gonna screw things up like she does. Like I can't even be different from her. I guess Zachary is just like everybody.

"And what about you?" I say. This can't be all about me.

"Me?" he says. "Yeah, especially me. You inherited some bad genes all around."

"Then don't yell at me, if it's your fault."

"You're hanging with the wrong crowd. You need new friends."

"She's not my friend. I just met her a couple of days ago."

"Then why would you risk your life for her doing something stupid like that?"

"I don't know." I really don't.

That seemed to shut him up. Or did he just decide it wasn't worth talking to me? We are pulling on to the 10 freeway, heading west; maybe he's concentrating on driving. No, the freeway's clear, and he's still staring straight ahead. He thinks I'm lying to him. So what? He can think what he likes. We don't need to talk. It's better if we don't. Just one thing I have to say.

"Why are you tripping on me? You don't think I can take care of myself? I've been taking care of myself ever since you left me with her."

"You were court ordered to live with her."

"Why? 'Cause you were such a screw-up? Maybe you think I'm just like her. And you think I'm just like you. Well maybe I'm not. Did you ever think of that? That maybe I can friggin' think for myself?"

"Don't get hurt. Please." The street lights are shining off that scar on his cheek. He still won't look at me. "Please," he repeats.

"Okay, but you could have said that last year, or the year before that, or the year before that, or the year before that, or..."

He interrupts me by just looking at me. We drive in silence a few miles, past the 405, into Santa Monica.

"You can live with me. I can fight her for full custody."

"What? Why would I?" And why am I letting him get to me, even talking about this?

"With your mom gone, I thought..."

"Take me home, Zachary."

"The judge gave me responsibilities."

"Good for you. But I'm not yours to keep."

He's quiet again. Who knows what he's thinking? I'm certainly not going to look at him right now to find out. Maybe we can keep up the not talking.

I scan the songs on Jade's iPod, Radiohead, Oasis, Incubus. Not too bad. Then he surprises me by turning on the radio. He flips around a little, finally settling on an old Red Hot Chili Peppers song. But I'm not gonna change it, not right now. I pocket Jade's iPod, lean my head on the door and close my eyes, riding along inside the black whale, wallowing in the song.

Chapter Twenty-six

S hut the hell up!"

Something crashes. I wake up. What? Outside. Another crash. Grunts, and more cursing. Neighbors fighting out on their balcony? Gleeson fighting with her husband?

"Again, and I make you go away in that dumpster," someone shouts. Then a big scuffle. It's like it's right outside the window, but my bedroom overlooks the ocean. No dumpsters anywhere near.

Unless, I am not in my bed.

Where am I? I bolt up and look around. The streetlamp outside shines on a wall with about a hundred guitars. Shit, it's Zachary's bedroom. How'd he get me in here? I must have fallen asleep in the limo. Did he carry me in like I was a baby or something? But it wasn't like that. I remember now, I walked in myself, I was so tired I wasn't thinking straight. He said he wasn't trying to keep me, just trying to obey the law and look out for me. What the judge asked him to do. So I let him. But only tonight. I know I said 'only tonight.' I was just waiting till he left so I could bail, but I guess I fell asleep.

I get off the bed, still in my clothes and sneakers and grab my pack and skateboard. I open the bedroom door into the living room. It's super creepy in here at night with all those damn statues. I look around for him. He's not anywhere. He's got a huge clock mounted on the wall. It looks like it's from some old train station. It probably is. It says it's 4:07. I walk up to the front door. There is a note taped to it:

Kal,
Don't leave.
Go back to sleep.
I have to work all night.
I'll be back before you go to school.
- Z

The writing is blocky and neat, all optimistic and assertive up-strokes and full round 'O's. Jeez, cop school is messing with me: I'm looking at the note the way they taught us in graphology. Anyway, nice note, but it won't stop me. I open the front door.

Flashing lights, a cop car approaching, siren wailing. The fight is still going on somewhere nearby.

I'm guessing it's not a great time to leave, not on a skateboard in the middle of the night in front of cops. I already got arrested once for that. And it's not going to kill me to stay the night. Even if it does look like half the statues and masks and surgical instruments are just waiting to jump me.

I fall back on the sofa and turn on the TV. It's set to DVD and there's a concert movie playing. An old Lollapalooza. Zachary must have been watching it. My mom is on stage singing with her band. And there right next to her is this skinny guy on lead guitar. He looks like he's about to fall over, all vacant eyes and twitches. But he's playing like a demon, inspired. It's Zachary, it must be.

He looks so different now. He's not as skinny and his eyes are more relaxed. It doesn't even seem like the same guy. But I know it is.

I must have been about two years old. I wonder where I am? Probably backstage with one of those ratty groupie girls.

It's weird to think how many times I walked by this building and never knew Zachary lived here. Maybe I even skated past him on the Boardwalk. Now he's talking about me moving in here. Where would I sleep?

If I had lived with him instead of my mom how different would my life have been? It's clear he doesn't have a lot of money. I definitely wouldn't have traveled as much or had all the clothes my mom bought for me.

The song on the DVD is over and Zachary leans over and kisses my mom tenderly like he really likes her. She acts all insecure like she does after she performs. But his kiss seems to strengthen her. She turns towards the camera and lets out a joyous wail. I pull one of Zachary's sweatshirts over me like a blanket and watch the DVD of my mom and dad performing together until I fall asleep again.

Chapter Twenty-seven

'm in line with Zachary at Intelligentsia's Venice Coffeebar on Abbot Kinney Boulevard. Apparently he takes his joe seriously. Otherwise why would we be standing outside waiting for coffee at six thirty-three in the morning?

The line is out the door... and down the narrow ramp that leads to the street. Next to the ramp, built-in benches are already half-filled, mostly Venice hipsters and yoga freaks. Zachary's t-shirt is black and faded and says: 'Venice: Where Art Meets Crime.' He's also wearing jeans and flip-flops. Everybody in Venice wears jeans and flip-flops.

"I turned in the limo," he tells me. "I don't want to be seen driving the beast anymore. I told them at the shop to swap out the license plate too. That was some night."

"Yeah. I never skitched a gangsta's ride before."

"Well, you've been lucky, I'm guessing."

"You always drive big beasts like that?"

"I've had that one for about a year, mostly proms and bachelorette parties. I'll get the occasional airport pickup."

"You like driving nights?"

"I'm an insomniac, so, yeah. Helps with the sobriety if I am busy at night. And most of the time my clients are fried, so that helps, reminds me how stupid it looks."

"I can't sleep either. Definitely not a morning person." I yawn a little to illustrate.

"I swapped the beast for a Lincoln Town car, and the day shift. Starting Monday I'll be driving rich Beverly Hills housewives around for awhile."

I know what that means. 'The day shift.' He'll have more time to spend with me. Oh, god.

The line moves pretty fast and we're greeted by a barista who leads us around to her station. All the baristas at this place have to wear white shirts and vests, like they're at a fancy restaurant or something. At the same time, they are tattooed and pierced, but this one especially.

"Hey, Zach."

"Hey Jessica, this is my daughter, Kali."

She looks at Zachary irritated, like he's been keeping a secret from her. "I didn't know you had a kid." Oh no, maybe they're hooking up.

"Yep. This is my kid." He looks at me like he's proud or something. It surprises me so I'm not quite ready with one of my smiles. That, and it's way too early for emotions, even fake ones.

She doesn't seem to care what my name is or who I am. She just wants to talk coffee with Zachary.

"Did you ever figure out the temperature of your porto filter?"

"I know, I know."

"Then I can't grind the beans for you here, Zachary. We've

been over this."

All I can think of is what are those things on her arm, on the thin pale skin of her inside forearm? Wait a minute, they're not on her skin, they're under it. Like those bugs that lay their eggs under your skin and hatch and scratch their way out. Except these are star shaped, five sided. Maybe they're starfish bugs.

"Teflon," Jessica says, holding out her arm to show me. "It's non-reactive."

They're so creepy. "Can I touch one of them?"

She didn't expect that, but her arm is out to me, like she's giving blood, so she nods. I touch one, and the skin slides over the Teflon. Very slippery. The little star pushes the skin up at least a quarter inch. I wiggle it around a little, slowly. That's too much for her, and she pulls back. I give her my big 'you rock' smile. It works, as usual, and she smiles back. She turns to Zachary, back in her groove.

"Double?"

"Yeah, perfect." He gives her a giant grin.

Oh, help me, they're flirting. "Can I get a soda?" I interrupt.

"We don't have soda here. Don't you drink coffee?" asks Jessica.

"Don't you drink coffee?" echoes Zachary.

"No."

That stops them, so I help them out: "Chai Latte."

I watch Jessica make Zachary's coffee with nice, smooth precision. But I can't stop staring the implants in her forearms. She's also got stars tattooed on both sides of her neck up to under her ears. If it weren't for all the stars, she'd look like a cheerleader with her blond ponytail bouncing around.

She hands Zachary his cappuccino lovingly, like it's her pet hamster. He proudly shows me the heart shaped swirl at the top of the foam.

"Coffee art. Jessica's the master, I mean the mistress, I guess." He winks at her and puts a dollar bill in her tip jar. Jessica hands me my latte. We find a place to sit on one of the benches along the ramp at the entrance. I pick up a fallen New York Times, and look at the headlines. That's when I notice today's date: it's Friday.

Friday, 9:00 P.M. Attic. Marley.

What the hell am I gonna do about that? I start thumbing through the paper. Here's something: some guy had his throat removed for cancer and has to learn all new ways to communicate. Maybe I could pretend I can't talk, see how that goes.

"Ahhh, good coffee," says Zachary.

I nod. I don't even look up. How do you tell someone you aren't going to talk, without talking?

"How do you know Jade again? She a friend of yours?"

He's acting like I'm not even reading. I shake my head, no.

"Then why did you go risking your neck to help her?"

Talk, talk, talk. I close the paper. I try my 'I don't know' look.

"Do you know anything about this guy Frankie? Would you say he is likely to come after us? Me?"

I've got no clue. I shrug.

"It's not every day a gang banger is bangin' on my car

door, even if I do live in Venice. Maybe I should talk to the police."

Okay, time to talk. "I thought you didn't do police. Jade doesn't want the cops involved."

"I don't know, Kal."

"I'll find out more today. I promise. Just don't call the cops." I change the subject. "When do you see Marley again?"

"Not for another month."

"A month!?"

"Once a month is all I can see her. You shouldn't even know about her. I'm not supposed to introduce her to family members."

"Why?"

"Can't allow yourself to get too involved with the kids otherwise they'll want to move in with you and you'll want them to move in. It's hard to stay objective."

So does this mean he won't get too involved with me? Am I just another case to him? Good reminder: keep my distance.

"We better go." Zachary downs the rest of his joe. I grab my backpack. Zachary picks up my skateboard. We walk out onto the sidewalk and he starts spinning my wheels.

"You're not going to stop skitching just because I ask you to, are you?"

"No."

"You need better cruising trucks, with bigger wheels."

Where's all this coming from? What does he know? Anyway, I like how light my rig is now. On the other hand, he's got a point. Venice Boulevard was rough.

"What are you doing after school?"

"Babysitting." It's true, I watch Stella every Friday

afternoon. "And all night too." I throw that last part in to buy myself time to figure out this Marley thing.

"You are hard to schedule," he says, very seriously. Then he hands me a key. "It's a spare, to my apartment. Don't lose it, use it." I stick the key in my pocket. Then he asks, "have to be somewhere right now?"

"School." Why did I admit that? Sometimes I can't think straight talking to him.

"You know how to run?" he asks me, very serious. I'm not sure what to say. He drops my board on the sidewalk and steps on it with his left leg.

"Run," he says. "It's easy: like you're pushing with both legs. Not as easy as skateboarding, but you'll figure it out."

He pushes hard with his right leg and hops on. He rolls down Abbot Kinney along the sidewalk, weaving through the people, past the trendy shops and restaurants, smooth as a snake.

And here I am running fast as I can to catch up.

Chapter Twenty-eight

I didn't think you'd be at school today," I tell Jade as we walk towards the corner window in the science lab. "Here's your iPod."

She takes it. "Why not?"

"I thought you'd be too scared to show your face."

We settle down in the corner and put a box of supplies down on the counter under the window.

"I'm not scared."

"Are you kidding? Yesterday, Frankie, hello?"

"He didn't even pull a piece."

"If he did, you'd be scared?"

"If? You aren't used to having a cousin break into your bathroom, are you? When you're shaving your legs in the shower and rub the nozzle of his gun in your left eye and call you a... pass the talcum." She pulls on a pair of rubber gloves.

Shit. I pass the talcum. "So what happened?"

"Not sure, but he must have hit me, 'cause I woke up on the bottom of the tub with the shower still on, but on cold. And a bad black eye for weeks, and I was shivering almost as long."

"For real?" I believe her; I just don't know what to say.

"Girl, you don't know what my life is like." She sprinkles talcum powder on a windowsill. We're dusting for fingerprints.

I take a big soft brush and start brushing the powder gently off the sill. "So, what, is Frankie in an L.A. gang?"

She rightly sneers at me because it's a stupid question.

"Put on your gloves first."

"Sorry, my bad." She ignores me. I pull on a set of tight rubber gloves.

"Why is this your business?"

"Maybe 'cause I only almost got killed last night because of you."

"You only almost got killed because of your own stupid-ass fault. Not mine. You didn't have to follow me. Why don't you concentrate on forensics?"

Jade focuses on the dusting and pretends to ignore me. Then she pipes up suddenly, "My mom moved us from the Midwest 'cause me and my brother were recruited by the gangs there. She wanted a fresh start for us."

"Guess that plan failed."

"As soon as we get to L.A. then Frankie leans on me to be a drug mule."

Jade's talking really quietly. She keeps looking around to see if anyone else is listening. But they aren't. The rest of the dweebs are paired up all over the middle of the classroom. We're the only ones in the corner.

"They wanted me to carry drugs for them from L.A. to China."

"Did you have to swallow condoms with coke or

something?" I read about that on NewYorkTimes.com.

"Not yet, but they filled condoms with sugar and forced me to swallow them, just to practice." Jade hops up onto the counter.

"No shit?" I've heard about this too.

Jade throws some powder onto the molding around the window. It falls down on top of me. I brush it out of my hair.

"You'd be the perfect mule for an Asian run. Nobody would suspect you were carrying drugs."

"Exactly what they think, but not for that reason. They have cheaper ways to get the drugs there. But my job is what they call executive elite. I deliver the stuff directly to the customer, usually some fancy hotel. With no middlemen, it's considered safer. And of course the girl–that would be me–is considered a 'delicacy' by the customer, and I'm expected to behave like a 'delicacy.'"

I kneel on the counter below the window ledge and follow her powdering with my brush. "So what happened to your brother?" I'm not sure I should ask this, but I can't help myself.

"My brother was protecting me, he gets in Frankie's face and there's this fight... It's just me and my mom now."

"Unbelievable. He killed his own cousin?"

She puts down the powder.

"He doesn't care."

I sit on the counter.

"Thanksgiving dinner at your house must suck."

"When my family gets together any time, it sucks." She sits next to me.

"What do they think of you going to cop school?"

"They're concerned for my mental health. But I'm hoping being around cops twenty-four-seven, I might stand a chance."

"I'm a crook," barks Officer Mendoza, appearing suddenly behind us. "What do I touch?"

We both jump.

"Young ladies, less talk, more fingerprints. Drop and give me twenty." Groaning, we get down on the floor and do twenty push-ups while Mendoza counts. The other dweebs look over at us. When we're through, Jade stands up first and offers me a hand up.

Mendoza hands Jade a pack of finger print cards and then moves on.

"Does Mendoza know?" I ask as Jade rips open the cards.

"Not until you blabbed about my tats."

"Did he say anything about it?"

"No, but he's not the problem right now."

"What's the problem, now?"

"I just wish my mom could afford protection money."

"What happened to Frankie?"

Jade pulls a couple of cards out of the pack.

"The Range Rover he was driving was stolen. He just walked away from it and was gone by the time the cops came. He'll come around again."

I think about what Zachary said. About calling the cops... maybe he's right. So I ask her, "Should we go to the cops?"

She shakes her head from side to side slowly, like she wants to but it's way beyond her control. "I tried that once. I even met the cops, spent an afternoon at the station, told them what was going on. That night, at dinner, Frankie asks me about it."

"How did he find out? Was he following you?"

"He knew exactly everything I told the cops."

"Dirty cop?"

"Frankie explained it to me real clear that night. He explained he has a bunch of friends on the force. That's the night he beat me in the shower."

This doesn't sound good. I'm wondering how much I should tell Zachary. I mean it was his limo that caused Frankie to crash. But the limo was turned in and the plates switched. The windows were dark so Frankie couldn't have seen what Zachary looks like. I'm sure he's safe. But if something happens to Zachary, it's gonna be my fault. Now I am starting to panic a little so I start thinking really fast. "You got any evidence on Frankie that would put him away for good for murdering your brother?"

"Like the ten people who saw him do it? Not a chance. They'd have to testify."

"What if we sneak in his house? Find the murder weapon and then get his fingerprints."

"We'd never get past his pit bull."

"We'll poison his pit bull."

Jade starts laughing. "You're crazy. Skitching on a gangsta's car? Who does that?"

She presses a fingerprint card against the windowsill then peels it back... revealing fingerprints.

"Officer Mendoza, sir," she shouts, all excited like a kid finding candy. "We got a hit. Two prints!"

Chapter Twenty-nine

Totally incredible. Damn. You should talk to the cops. This is some serious shit."

Penn is all heated up. We're outside our school lined up at Dogtown Dogs food truck.

"Jade said no cops." I'm trying to be as serious as he is.

"You shouldn't get involved with Jade."

"I am involved." I step up to the window of the truck and look into the full kitchen inside. "Tots with Cheese," I order.

"Don't be stupid. She's an ex-gang member. You need to be careful." He turns to the order guy. "Give me a Spicy Angelino."

"I'm super careful," I tell him.

"You take it easy. And just walk away from that gang shit." Jeez, lighten up, Mr. Lawyer.

"What do you care?"

"Just walk away."

"Sure, whatever."

Now he's checking his phone and outright ignoring me. He looks like I hurt his feelings. Does he have any clue how much lawyers don't make me warm and fuzzy, the bastards always 'dealing with me' when my mom's away?

I snap my fingers in front of his phone. "Rude."

He glances down at me like I'm an annoying kid. Can't have that, so I throw him one of my smiles, not too heavy. I have to watch it; how many times have I ended up in the wrong place in the morning because of the smile? But he squints like he knows it's fake.

"Aren't you ever serious?" he asks me.

Is it possible he can tell the real smile from the bullshit one? If he can, good for him; not too many people can. I mean, it's true he doesn't seem to be like other lawyers: he's incredibly yummy, for one. Did I say that out loud? No. I don't think I did, but it's bad enough I thought it. If he can tell which smile is real, maybe he can read my mind and hears me thinking he's yummy.

"How long does it take to make some god damn Tots with Cheese?" I said that out loud, I'm pretty sure.

He puts his phone away. "Almost forgot," he says, "I got something for you."

He's digging around in his backpack and hands me a paperback book. It's called: *RASTAFARI: Itations of Jamaica and I* with a photo of a beautiful Rasta woman on the front wearing dreadlocks.

"What's this for?"

"You spent all that money to get your hair done. You don't even know what it means. Rastafarianism is a religion. Rastas dread their hair. It's a ritual, a symbol. It's accepting a religion for God's sake, not some fad that can get you into the Roxy at night."

"I don't need my hair to get me into a night club."

"Oh, excuse me. I forgot who I was talking to."

"I know what Rastas are."

"Yeah. Well, listening to Bob Marley doesn't cut it. Just read the book. Recognize what you represent."

The order guy hands me my tater tots and Penn his Spicy Angelino, all beef dog wrapped in bacon with spicy pico de gallo and jalapeno peppers.

We walk back over the big brown lawn in front of the school and sit down on the dry grass. The lawn is littered with students eating lunch.

"How come you know so much about Rastas?" I study his closely cropped hair.

"This isn't about me."

"Sounds like it is."

"My dad's Jamaican. I half grew up in that culture."

"Is your mom?"

He's looking at a bunch of senior girls laughing. A little smile erupts in his eyes. I can't believe he's checking them out so in my face. But he says: "No, she's all little white church with a steeple filled with white people. My dad was her spring break mistake."

Just then Jade comes up to us.

"Hi. Who's this?" she says.

"I'm Penn."

"He's my lawyer. He's supposed to be coming up with a plan to get me out of cop school. This is Jade, she's my partner in crime school." Jade takes some of my tots.

"Hello, Jade," he says with a mouth full of Spicy Angelino. I'm hoping Penn won't tell Jade I told him about her and Frankie so I throw him this look that says, "Don't friggin'

144

talk." He gets the look and throws one back at me that says, "Don't tell me what to say and not say." He turns back to Jade, "So you gonna be a cop when you grow up?"

"Something like that. You gonna be a lawyer?"

"That's the plan. What about you, Kal, you gonna be a criminal?"

Jade and Penn both laugh. I hate that, more than anything, when people laugh at me, but somehow these two make me laugh too.

"Tell me you never got in trouble, Penn," I say.

He picks up both hands in front of him like he's innocent, "I haven't."

"Never?"

"Nope."

"Not once. Never arrested?"

"Nope."

"Expelled from school?"

"No."

"Suspended?'

"Uh, uh."

"Sent to the office?" Jade offers.

"Not even in kindergarten."

"That's impossible, nobody's that perfect," I say.

"Ladies, cast your eyes on perfection." Oh brother, is he for real? Then I notice Jade. She's giggling at him, she thinks he's charming. What the? And now he's throwing a big smile her way. I've got to do something here. But what am I thinking? Why do I care if they're into each other? Put it in check, Kal. In check.

Penn turns to me and says, "So what about this girl you

wanted to get into Teen Court. You got any info on her yet?"

"Yeah, I'm gonna meet her tonight. Off Main Street in Venice. A party or something. Around nine o'clock."

"You have curfew at nine o'clock. Did you forget that?"

"No, I know that, but give me a break. You a narc now too?"

"That the only time she can meet?"

"Yeah, she's like this foster kid. She's always moving from house to house." I am totally making all this up. Where it's headed, I have no idea.

"All right. I'll meet you there." He stands up. "Give me the address."

That's a surprise, but I won't refuse. I don't know what I'm getting into with Marley and maybe it would be good to have Penn there. I reach in my pocket and pull out the magazine corner that Marley gave me with the address and toss it to Penn.

Then Penn turns to Jade and says, "You gonna be there?"

"No," I say. But Jade is answering at the same time, smoothly, without even looking at me.

"Yeah, think I will."

I look at Penn then at Jade and I get it.

"Later, ladies." And with his hands in his pockets and a nod to each of us, he moves off.

I should tell Jade she's not invited. I should definitely not get her involved with this whole Marley thing, but here I am doing it, not saying anything, letting her come. She knows what I'm thinking, I can tell, because she grins, takes my last tater tot and eats it with a shrug.

Chapter Thirty

We're deep in designer shoes and boots. Gleeson's helping me look for a pair of black shine-able boots that I can wear with my dress uniform during inspection at police school. She told me she has the perfect pair so we're digging around in her ginormous walk-in closet.

"Here they are," she says pulling a boot box out from under a huge stack of shoeboxes. "I only wore them once." Out comes a pair of Dries Van Noten boots. They're shiny and black, combat style. Perfect to polish.

"Are you sure?" I ask. "These are like $3,000 boots." I know 'cause my mom wore a pair just like them in her *Get Real* video. Only my mom and I don't have the same shoe size like me and Gleeson do.

"Sure it's fine, I got them on sale." Still on sale must be a couple of grand. I try them on while Gleeson digs through her shoe collection. She slips on a pair of high stilettos and walks around the closet. She stops in front of the full length mirror. "Do my calves look bigger to you?"

"Huh?" I'm not really paying attention to her, just trying to lace up the boots, which fit perfectly. They've got a steel heel and they lace up the front. The laces thread through the heel. I could really hurt a perp if I kicked one with these boots on.

There's no question they're awesome boots, but if I wear these I'll for sure stand out more than I already do.

I spot a pair of beat up boots in the corner. "How about those?" I point.

"My punk rock boots?" Gleeson holds up a pair of old black Doc Martins and inspects them. She walks over and shows me the bottom of one of them. A small round mark is in the sole. "This is where I'd put my cigarettes out. I tried to burn a hole all the way through, but the sole's too thick. Made of petroleum, but it doesn't burn, doesn't even melt." She hands them to me. "Try 'em on."

They fit like a pair of old blue jeans. "I like these."

"I don't know, Kal." She sits down next to me and strokes the boots like a kitten. "I'm not sure I'm ready to part with them."

"It's okay," I tell her as I take them off.

"You sure you don't want the Van Noten's?"

"I love then, but I don't think I can really wear them to school."

"Take 'em if you want, if not I'll try and sell them on Ebay." She always says that about her things, selling them on Ebay, but she never does.

"Mommmmmmy," Stella calls for her from the other room.

"Can you go see what she wants, Kal?"

I wander into the kitchen and see that Stella has spilled a whole bag of dried spaghetti all over the floor.

"What's wrong Stella?"

"Pasta broke." She's crying a little.

"It's okay, baby. Pasta breaks. See." I sit down next to her, take a hand full of the spaghetti and break it in half. Then I sprinkle it on the ground next to her. I hand her some more. "You try." She takes it from me and hesitantly breaks a little. When she does, I laugh and so does she. She's so cute when she laughs. She's got a tiny face with big lips. I think she's really cute, but I don't think Gleeson thinks so. She was looking at her sleeping one day and said 'look at those giant lips, at least she's not gonna need collagen.' I like Gleeson a lot but she is so into appearances. You can't get away from it in L.A. Boob jobs, face-lifts, I'm surrounded by it. Even Gleeson keeps telling me I should get your first facelift in your late twenties.

I start to pick up the pasta when Gleeson appears in the doorway in a bathing suit. She's pulling on a kimono robe. She doesn't care about the mess in the kitchen. "The maid will clean it up. You ready?"

I stand up, reach for Stella's hand and we go out into the hallway of the condo. The elevator door opens, revealing that amazing view of the ocean through the back of the elevator like we're flying up the coast. The elevator is definitely my favorite part of this building. We lower down to the pool level.

"So after my swimming lesson, I'm going to see my life coach. You can stay till eight right?"

"Yeah, no prob." Gleeson's life coach thinks Gleeson should become a life coach, but Gleeson has never had a job her whole life and isn't about to start now. Her little girl holds my hand while Gleeson puts on her bathing cap.

We get down to the pool and Gleeson dives in, joining six women in matching bathing suits. Stella and I sit on the edge of the pool and splash our toes in the water. We watch as the women swim in unison then flip on their backs and form a circle. They each lift up one leg and skull around the circle. Synchronized swimming.

My phone pings with a text from Dakota: HANG 2NITE?

How am I gonna do that? I never told him about this thing with Marley. And I never told him about Jade and I really never told him about Penn. I can't have the two of them meet. Dakota will just rag on me for hanging with a wanna-be lawyer type.

So I text him back: BABYSITTING ALL NIGHT. He'll probably think this is a lie 'cause Gleeson never asks me to babysit all night and he knows it. Stella pulls my hand towards the Jacuzzi.

I strip to my bikini. Stella tugs at my belly button ring. I push her hand away and then me and Stella splash into the Jacuzzi. She spits water at me. I splash her back. She starts playing with the jets and I sink back into the bubbles and it's quiet for a frickin' second. I look out across the pool to the Santa Monica Mountains on one side and the ocean on the other and think about how different my life is from Jade's.

Chapter Thirty-one

Almost nine o'clock and I'm waiting in front of twenty-four-foot-tall binoculars. The entrance to a building across the street from the one I'm supposed to meet Marley at. The whole weird building was designed by the architect Frank Gehry and it's in half the pictures you see of Venice. The binoculars were done by the artist, Claes Oldenburg. I'm sitting on the high cement ledge in front texting Zachary: SLEEPING AT GLEESON'S TONIGHT–BABYSITTING. There goes the lie again, but he's all in my face wanting to know where I am even though he didn't give a damn for the last seven years.

"Owww." I put my hand down too hard on the ledge and it lands on one of those metal pieces they drill into cement edges to stop skateboarders like me from grinding on them. I shake out my hand as an orange MTA bus drops off Jade.

She's wearing skinny jeans and a big grey sweatshirt that says: CALSTATE NORTHRIDGE. Her hair is down, tucked behind her ears. She moves smoothly, slowly. Her eyes are busy scanning the block. We don't have any time to talk before Penn rides his Vespa onto the driveway that runs right under the binoculars.

"This the place?" he asks. He scooters in a figure eight around the binoculars.

"No." I say and point to a rundown three-story building across the street. The two of them turn to look.

Penn parks his Vespa in front of a new green VW Beetle and locks his helmet in the compartment under his seat.

"Punch buggy no punch backs," Jade says and she hits me in the arm, hard. Nobody older than seven plays that game, the one where you hit someone when you see a VW Beetle. My arm hurts, but I don't show it. I ignore her. The three of us walk across the street and down a walk street. Venice has a bunch of these streets near the beach where it's just sidewalk down the middle. No cars can drive on them.

We stand in front of the building and Penn says, "Doesn't look like a party in there." He's right; the house is really dark and quiet.

I walk up to the front door and try the handle. "It's locked." I point out a couple of bright lights coming from the attic window. "Something's going on up there. Maybe we enter around the back."

We walk down around to the back alley. It's pretty quiet. Just a couple of cats that scatter at the sight of us. And an old Beetle is parked tight up against a fence. I see it first.

"Punch buggy no punch backs," I say as I hit Jade in the arm, hard as she did. She smiles a little.

There's a back door up at the top of a flight of stairs. We climb up and check the door. It's locked too.

"Should we knock?" asks Penn, but he doesn't want to any more than Jade and I.

I look up and see a fire escape within reach. I point, "Up here."

Penn is jumpy; he says under his breath, "I don't think this is a good idea. There might be consequences. We should know what we're getting ourselves into."

"She said the attic."

I lead the way up the fire escape. They follow me. It's rusty as hell but it's not collapsing so we keep climbing.

We all make it to the top and peer into the attic window. The blind is down, but there's a one-inch gap at the bottom and the window is just wide enough for all three of us to look in: inside is a forest of movie lights and other movie set equipment. There are bounce cards sprouting from C-stands, big flat panels of white fabric on some of them, shiny tinfoil on others. The C-stands are the trees of the movie set forest, adjustable metal poles that everything gets attached to. It's a big loft with high sloping ceilings following the roof-line. There are a few people; one guy must be the cameraman, adjusting a video camera. He's small and thin, all in black, with black hair and a thin soul patch under his thin lips. There's a grip, twenty-something, with a shaved head. He's also lean, but strong, in a tight T-shirt that shows off his muscles and big belt of tools that seems about to pull his jeans down. He's up on a ladder, stapling a cable to the top of the bedroom wall. Which is part of the set. They've built a whole bedroom inside the loft. Another guy, older and heavier, with long graying hair, is rolling a light on a C-stand across the room. Maybe he's the DP, the director of photography. Penn whispers: "A low-budget video?"

"Why would Marley want us to see this?" I say.

"Where is she, anyway?" Jade asks.

"Quiet," whispers Penn.

The three of us watch for a few minutes and still no Marley.

A window at the end of the fire escape opens. It's down at the far end of the room, behind the bedroom set. The three of us plaster ourselves against the side of the house. A hand holding a cigarette pops out of the window followed by a head and a cloud of smoke. The smoke clears and I can see the head belongs to Roseanne, Marley's foster mom. I actually bite my lip to stop from saying anything. She sucks and blows smoke for a bit. Someone from inside yells: "Makeup." Roseanne quickly stubs her cigarette out in an empty flowerpot and pulls her head back inside the house. She leaves the window open.

I look back through the gap in our window and see Roseanne waddle across the room carrying make-up brushes and other make-up paraphernalia in a big plastic zip-lock bag. She goes behind a red and gold folding Chinese screen. "Marley," she calls in a sickening sing-song voice.

Marley appears from what looks like the bathroom. She walks slowly across the room, holding two cups of coffee. Nobody's paying any particular attention to her, which isn't surprising, since she's following a twenty something woman who is naked. Completely naked. Marley is dressed at least in shorts and a tank top.

"Is that her?" Jade hisses, suddenly very tense.

"Yeah, oh shit."

And now there's a guy walking out from behind the set on the other side of the room. He's handsome, like a male model, and walks like he's modeling on the runway. Which is crazy, since he's also naked. Marley hands them both the coffee cups. Then the guy hands Marley a joint he's been smoking. She takes a hit.

"Marley's how old?" Penn asks.

"Twelve," I whisper.

"This is some bad shit," says Jade very cold.

"She shouldn't be here," Penn whispers back.

"It's good I'm not carrying a weapon," Jade mutters, "I want to kill them." She is furious, scary furious.

"I think we should leave, call the cops," Penn whispers.

Jade says, "No cops." For someone who's in cop school, what's her problem with cops?

"I don't know," I say. I mean I'm sure Penn is right, but we're trespassing, I'm breaking curfew, we don't even really know Marley...

"I'm getting her out," Jade snaps.

"Cool it," Penn insists. "Don't get all emotional now."

Jade glares at us both and speaks very deliberately: "You want to see emotional? I'm going in through the window."

"What? Are you crazy?" I say.

"Hey, she wanted you to come, no?" says Jade.

"It's too dangerous." Good point, Penn.

"Kal, you and me will go in first," says Jade, ignoring him. "We'll sneak behind the Chinese screen, to Marley. Penn, you keep those creeps off us. Kal, you take Marley back out this window and down the fire escape. Leave the fat lady to me. Let's go."

"Jade, you're over reacting," Penn objects, but Jade is already heading along the fire escape to the open window. Me and Penn are right behind her.

Jade dives head-first through the open window, tucking and rolling and coming up running. I climb in right behind her and run after her, around the back of the set. Somebody shouts; I guess they saw us, but we make it to the folding Chinese screen and look behind it. Marley looks up at me and her eyes light up.

"You came. That's so cool." She pops her gum.

"Zachary's kid?" Roseanne screeches. "What the hell are you doing here?" She goes white in the face, her lips thin and tight.

"I invited her," grins Marley, blowing a bubble.

"This is a closed set, Marley," says Roseanne, shaking a little, reaching into her purse. I don't know what she's got in there, but I bet it's a gun... Penn obviously thinks so too, 'cause he kicks the purse to the floor and picks it up quickly.

"Marley, let's get out of here." My voice sounds tense.

Roseanne screeches again: "It's a kidnapping! Stop them!" She's panting for air, out of breath.

I reach out my hand to Marley, but Roseanne grabs her other hand. Jade runs at Roseanne, knocking her hand away from Marley. Roseanne sits heavily on the ground, where she stays, grunting and wheezing. I run with Marley towards the window. The cameraman is backing away, but the grip on the ladder has clambered down quickly, pulling a hammer out of his belt.

"Who are you?" he asks me.

"Who are *you*, jerk?" I yell at him. "She's twelve. She shouldn't be here."

The grip hesitates.

"Twelve, bullshit." He looks at Marley. "You're eighteen,

right?"

"Not exactly," says Marley with a cute little grin. She holds up ten fingers and then closes her hands and holds up two more, showing him how old she is, just like a kid would.

"You gonna believe these gangsters?" gasps Roseanne. She's clutching her chest, sputtering with fury. "They're kidnapping my daughter!"

"They're my friends," says Marley.

The DP seems frozen, but he's blocking the way to the window. The grip is blocking the path around the set to the front door. For a moment everyone stops. We're trapped.

"Use the gun," yells Jade. "In the purse."

Penn looks at the purse he's still holding. He obviously does not want to do this, but he does: he reaches in... not what he expected... he looks in the purse and pulls out... an inhaler. He glances to Roseanne, and tosses her the inhaler. She shoves it in her mouth and breathes deeply. The DP is still blocking the window. Somebody should do something.

So I take out my cell phone, quickly opening the camera app. The naked man leaps off the bed–I snap a picture of him–and runs behind the set muttering "where's my pants?"

"Put that away!" the DP yells at me, pointing at my phone, rushing at me. I take a picture of him just as Penn pushes over a C-stand with a big movie light on it, right at the DP, who leaps to catch it, but misses and trips. It crashes loudly with a small explosion of broken glass. I try to step around it with Marley, but now the lean, muscled grip is blocking the way, sneering, moving towards us, his hammer raised. I try to take a picture of him, but he ducks, covering his face, giving me a chance to run away from him. Maybe this is getting out of control.

I'm holding Marley's hand and the DP is starting to get up again, grunting at me, a murderous look in his eye. He knocks over two big glasses of soda. I duck, but Marley gets soaked.

Penn grabs a bunch of cables on the floor and pulls hard, yanking a couple of other C-stands over; huge bounce cards and scrims fall around the grip. It doesn't stop him, but it distracts him for a moment so he doesn't see the sandbag Jade hurls at him... which catches him flat on the chest. He collapses to the ground, winded. Jade drops another sandbag on his head, dazing him.

I pull Marley to the attic window, trying to avoid tripping in the chaos. But the grip is relentless, up again, and coming for us with a screwdriver in his hand. Jade rushes up from behind him, swings a leg around in a wide arc and kicks him in the balls. He collapses to the ground.

"Awwww shitttt," he screeches some sick noise like an amp with a short. The naked man runs out from the other side of the set, still with no pants.

The DP is back up. He's swinging a C-stand over his head and running at us. Penn pushes the grip, who's still hunched over in agony, from behind, sending him into the DP, who stumbles into a C-stand holding more scrims. The whole thing falls in a clattering mess around him.

I'm helping Marley out the window; Jade follows us out, then I look back for Penn. He's trying to get to the window, but Roseanne's rushing at him. I guess she got her breath back.

"Behind you!" I yell at Penn. He drops and rolls on the ground, grabs a coil of cable and hurls it up at Roseanne. She dodges the flying cable, but trips on another cable on the floor, falling hard through a fabric wall of the scenery. The whole set begins a slow motion collapse, each wall pulling down the next, forcing the crew to run to avoid being crushed.

Penn clambers through the window and pulls it down, closed. So now we're all four on the fire escape. It's cold outside and Marley's clothes are completely soaked. Jade yanks off her sweatshirt–she's got a singlet on underneath–and quickly pulls the sweatshirt over Marley covering her like a dress. Jade is first down the rusty stairs, leading Marley. I glance back at the window. The crew is scrambling around, heading for the door at the far end of the room. The naked man has finally found his pants. I guess they've figured out it's smarter to get the hell out of there than come after us, so we make it down to the ground without trouble.

"Follow me," I yell, and we run down the alley to a side street. We turn right on Main Street and just keep running.

Chapter Thirty-two

I take the lead, Penn's behind me, then Marley and Jade. I make a beeline to Zachary's apartment, which is about seven blocks, running all the way. They follow me up the stairs, panting. I use the spare key Zachary gave me to get in. I know he's not home 'cause this is his last night at work before he switches to the day shift.

As soon as all of us are in, I close and lock the door.

"Marley, you okay?" I ask. We're all out of breath.

"Yeah, awesome getting me out of there. So totally not in the mood to do that anymore." It's weird that she's not upset or anything. She looks around the apartment, gazing at all the creepy art. "What is this place?"

"Zachary's apartment."

"Oh, no shit? Zachary lives here?" She's so casual.

"How long have they been shooting the movie?" I ask.

"Like a couple of months. They make different movies. Pretty much every Friday night."

"Have you ever been in one of their films, Marley?"

"No. Now I just help them get coffee and clean up. That sort of thing. Roseanne says maybe soon. I'm a pretty good actress."

She takes the crash test dummy off the swing, puts it on the floor and starts swinging like a little girl. Her feet brush the dummy as she swings over it. I'm relieved to hear they haven't used her in the films, but still, she shouldn't even be there.

Jade nervously looks out all the windows. She jiggles the door handle to make sure it's locked.

Penn walks over to Jade and says something to her quietly that I can't hear. She pulls away from him and I can see that she's crying.

"What's wrong?" I ask. Jade turns her head away from me. She looks over to Marley who is now curled up in a ball on the couch with the big sweatshirt pulled over her legs. She's playing with Zachary's fake stuffed rabbit.

"Those assholes are pissing me off. We should have taken the film too. That's what they're interested in, not her."

"I got it," Pen says as he pulls a mini DV cassette out of his pocket. "There was a camera on the ground. I popped it open and swiped the tape."

"They're gonna come after us for it," I say.

"Not if we turn it into the cops."

"Who said anything about the cops?" asks Jade.

"She's twelve, Jade. We're calling the cops. That's what you're supposed to do when someone is in danger." Penn is all heated up.

"Slow down, you two. Let's just think about this," I say.

Jade's looking around the room. She picks up the French condom mold from Zachary's collection and studies it. "What's this thing?" Jade asks, holding the mold up to the light.

I take it back from her. "It's a condom mold. From France."

"Why does your old man have a condom mold?" Penn takes it out of my hands, all interested now.

"How should I know?"

"I want to see." Marley jumps up off the couch, comes over to us and starts to check out the mold. "That's cool."

I sit down on the swing. Jade starts pushing me.

"I never swallowed a condom full of sugar," she says all quietly.

"What?" I turn around to look at her over my shoulder.

"Frankie's a pimp. He likes girls like Marley. You know, young."

"You working for him too?"

"Not yet. But that's what he wants."

"That's why you freaked out back there."

"I didn't freak. I stopped a crime. That's what cops do. What everybody should do when they can. That's why…"

"Okay, I get it," I interrupt. "We all agree. We were all there."

"Maybe Frankie wants you too, now," says Jade, looking at me with a steady gaze.

"Why me?" I stop the swing.

"Why not? You're cute, you're young, you tailed him on the Range Rover, he'll want to use you, control you. And he never forgets a face." I feel sick to my stomach. Jade goes on, more quietly: "I'm gonna kill him. I'm gonna learn everything I can in cop school and then kill him."

I laugh. Nobody else does. Jade is looking far away. She's serious.

"That's crazy," I tell her. "You'll spend the rest of your life in jail."

Now it's Jade's turn to laugh, though it's a freaky laugh with no humor in it. "What have I got to lose? It's not like I'm going to live past twenty-one anyway."

"I thought you wanted to be a cop."

"I want to believe being trained as a cop will help me protect myself, but who am I kidding?" She's wound up, her voice rising. "The gangs outnumber the cops and out-shoot them every day. Anyway, if I'm caught and sentenced to life for murder, I'll probably live longer than I would on the streets."

"She's right," says Penn. "But there's got to be a better way."

"I'll help you kill him," says Marley in a small voice from across the room. Marley has found the water pistol on Zachary's desk. She points it straight up and shoots, making a wet splotch on the ceiling. "Can we kill Roseanne too?"

"Hold on, nobody's killing anybody," says Penn.

"Roseanne deserves to die." Marley says, pointing the water pistol at Penn. "Bang, bang, bang!" She squirts Penn right in the eyes.

"Hey, cut that shit out," Penn pulls up his shirt to wipe off his face. Rad abs. Jade notices too.

Marley turns around and starts shooting Jade. But Jade grabs Marley's wrist and swings it behind her, throws Marley on her back and kneels over her, pinning her down.

"You're so dead, Marley," says Jade. I'm thinking Jade's lost her temper but she grabs the water pistol and shoots Marley with great splashes of water. Marley squeals with delight.

"Damn, girl, how'd you learn to throw somebody down like that?" Penn asks Jade.

"Cop school," Jade and I both say simultaneously.

"Jinx," Jade says quickly. Oh geez, another prepubescent game. Marley is laughing so hard now. Penn gives Jade a hand up.

"Kal, can I take a shower? I'm pretty sticky," asks Marley. "There, I un-jinxed you."

"Thanks." I say and help her to her feet. I walk Marley down the hallway and show her the bathroom. I give her a towel and find her an old t-shirt of Zachary's and a pair of sweat pants that look like they'll fit her.

When I come out into the living room I see Penn and Jade sitting on the sofa together. She's showing him the inside of her arms where she had her tattoos. He takes his finger and tenderly rubs it along the scar. She pulls her arm away quickly, not really trusting his touch. They both start laughing a little. I don't want to watch them. I want to get the hell out of here. But I can't just leave like I always do when I can't handle the situation. I can't just leave a bunch of people in Zachary's house. So I turn around and walk into his bedroom and lie down on the bed and stare at the wall of guitars and listen to the sounds on the street and the water falling down from the shower. And I feel the excitement of the night and the lump in my chest when I think of Jade sitting there where I should be.

I get a text from Dakota: RU STILL KIDSITTING?

I text back: YES.

Surprisingly, it's not a lie this time. Marley's only twelve.

Chapter Thirty-three

My moment of silence is broken by the sound of a door opening and closing. Feet scuffle around in the living room. I hear voices and one of them is Zachary's. What the hell is he doing home?

"Kal?" I hear him call.

I drag my body off the bed. I am not going to enjoy the next half hour of my life, I just know it.

Slowly I move to the door and watch through the crack. Luckily, he's showing off his art objects to Penn and Jade. Zachary doesn't look pissed that two teenagers are in his living room. He's enjoying the audience.

I open the door and brave it. I saunter into the room and plop down on the couch.

"Oh, hi," I say casually.

Zachary turns to me and, says, "I thought you were babysitting." He's not mad. He's acting like he got my plans wrong.

"Oh, yeah, well, it got cancelled."

"It's cool you brought your friends over."

It's all going pretty well until Marley comes out of the

bathroom with a towel around her head wearing his Red Hot Chili Peppers T-shirt and sweats.

"Oh, hey, Zachary." She plops down on the couch next to me acting like it's perfectly normal that she's sitting on his couch in wet hair wearing his clothes.

"Marley. What's going on? Why are you here?" He walks towards us.

I start to say something, but Marley interrupts, "I can't stay with Roseanne anymore. I need to get out of that house, Zachary, so I tracked you down and ran all the way. When I got here Kal and her friends were hanging out."

Man, she is quick with the lie. Zachary looks like he believes her. I look at Jade; she knows when to keep her mouth shut. It's Penn I'm worried about. He's all righteous and everything so I get ready to throw him one of my looks when he throws me one that says: *it's not cool*. He's right it's not.

"Is that my T-shirt?"

Marley nods and tugs at the center of the Chili Pepper's red asterisk logo on Zachary's shirt.

"She wanted to take a shower, so I found some of your clothes to wear."

"What happened to your clothes, Marley?"

Marley's not talking. Zachary looks around at all of us. It's pretty intense and we're listening carefully. Marley doesn't say a word. Then she takes one hand and pretends to zip her mouth shut.

"What's going on, Kal?" I open my mouth and nothing comes out. They're all looking at me.

"Somebody want to explain?" says Zachary. "Marley

knows whatever she tells me, I have to report to her social worker. Is that why you're not talking, Marley?" Marley nods and points at me. I still don't know what to say.

Penn jumps in, all the way: "We rescued Marley. From a porn shoot."

"What?" Zachary looks at me.

I nod. "Marley gave me a note in the cop shop the other night. Told me to meet her at a place on Dudley. We got there and she was serving coffee to this naked lady and there was this other dude who was naked."

Marley's on the swing now, pushing herself back and forth. I think she's relieved it's all coming out in the open.

"I wasn't naked, Zachary–" interrupts Marley.

"We should have called the police–" adds Penn.

"It was so cool, Zach," says Marley. "Like in the movies, like the A-Team rushing in to save me." Marley holds her two hands together, like she's holding a gun and swings her fake gun around towards all of us. She adds bullet sound effects. "Pow, pow, pow, pow."

The other two are talking over her really fast explaining to Zachary what happened.

Then Marley says, "Roseanne could barely breathe."

"Roseanne was there?" Zachary is startled. "Are you screwing with me? Marley, did Roseanne take you to a porn shoot?" Marley zips her mouth shut again, this time twisting her fingers like she's turning a key. Zachary's not taking it this time, though: he rushes over to her, kicking the dummy aside and blocking the swing. "Marley, why didn't you tell me about this?"

"Roseanne would kill me," Marley says quietly. "She said

so."

"I got their tape," says Penn. "Mini DV."

"I got pictures," I add. "Look." I hand him my phone and he scrolls through a few shots. He mutters angrily, shaking his head. Then strangely, he seems to calm down.

"We can't talk about this," he says. "Except to the cops."

"No cops," snaps Jade. "I'm not talking to cops."

"And your social worker, Marley," continues Zachary.

"No!" shouts Marley. "He's gonna put me back with Roseanne."

"Not after he sees these pictures."

"Can't I please just stay with you and Kal, Zachary?"

"You know the answer to that," he says softly. "But I'm glad you're here now."

Marley's eyes go wide and fill with tears. She slides off the swing, buries her head in her hands, and crumples into a ball on the floor beside the crash test dummy.

Zachary goes over to his desk and picks up his phone.

"Thanks, Kal, for bringing Marley here. You did the right thing." He dials.

Chapter Thirty-four

We're all at Ping's Place sharing a Chinese meal. Me, Marley, Jade, Zachary, Penn and Tiger's social worker, Evan. Evan is a tall black guy with big shoulders and a wide smile. He seems happy to be having a meal with Zachary. Marley barely looks at him; she's busy trying to pick up individual grains of rice with her chopsticks. It's super weird to be sitting here with all these people. I wish I wasn't here, but Zachary invited everybody after the cops left and interrogated everyone and what was I gonna do... say no?

"Come on, Marley. We gotta go," Evan says. "Say goodbye to your friends." Marley reluctantly gets up from the table and fist taps Penn and Jade. When she gets to me, she leans down and hugs me.

"I wish you could be my sister," she whispers. She stands up and says, "Bye Zachary. I'll see you Sunday, right?" He nods. She turns back to me, "Zachary's gonna take me to breakfast. Can you come too? Please?"

Evan interrupts before I can commit, "Come on, Marley, leave the girl alone. Let's get going."

"Bye, Kal."

"Bye."

I watch the two of them go off.

Jade pipes up, "Where's he taking her?"

"To a group home tonight until we can find her another placement. A safe placement."

"How long's that take?" asks Penn.

"For someone her age, could take a while. A lot of foster parents won't accept teens and pre-teens, think they're nothing but trouble."

"Like I am?" I ask.

"No, of course not," he says, but it sounds forced.

"Looks like the foster parents have their own problems," says Penn. "Judging by Roseanne."

"Luckily actual evil like that is rare in foster care."

"What happened to Marley's mom and dad?" asks Penn.

"Her idiot parents caught the house on fire one night. They were running a meth lab out in Riverside. Then they split but forgot to take the kids. So Marley and her little brother, Isaiah, were wandering around on their own for a couple of days. Somebody found them sleeping behind a dumpster at the elementary school."

"What happened to Isaiah?"

"A relative in Baker took him. Nobody wanted Marley, except for Roseanne, who was a distant cousin."

"She's a relative?" says Penn, astounded.

"Yep. Marley's been living with her for a couple of months. It makes me crazy to think what else had been going on in that house. I just got involved with her. This is all new to me."

"She acts like such a normal kid."

"She's got a great spirit."

"Why can't she stay with you?" I ask. "I don't get that."

"I'm not a registered foster parent. I work nights. I can't take care of a teenage girl."

Is he trying to tell me something? Is he implying... I look away from him. Does he think of me as a teenage girl? He's got enough going on. I'm just stressing him out and Marley needs his help more than I do.

"I gotta go pee," I tell them, although they're not listening to me. I squeeze out from behind the picnic-style table. The hallway to the bathrooms is close to the front door. Looking back I see that nobody's watching me so I turn and go out the front door; that wasn't the plan, it just seems like what I need to do. There's too much pressure back in there. Not pressure like anybody expects anything from me, more like I'm way deep underwater and the weight of the ocean is squeezing me from all sides. I know it doesn't make any sense.

It's loud outside on the street corner. There's a line to get into Ping's even though it's past midnight by now. The food isn't that great, I want to tell them. Across the street, a couple of tourists look out the windows of the Venice Youth Hostel, watching for local weirdness, probably. The neon lights in the window of the skateboard shop flicker below them. I walk over to the Big Blue Bus stop and sit on the fiberglass bench nestled between two movie posters promoting a horror movie with a big bloody hammer. I left my skateboard in Zachary's apartment. It would take me an hour to get back to my condo on foot. I look south on Pacific to see if there's a bus on the way. There isn't.

Victoria, Zachary's landlady, comes out of the restaurant.

She holds a cell phone and a pack of cigarettes. Her arms are weighted down with her gold bangly bracelets which jingle as she moves. She offers me her pack of Parliaments then plops down on the bench next to me.

"No, thanks," I say.

She lights up and then blows out a cloud of gray air.

"Tough night, huh?"

I just shrug. Not sure why she's all in my business.

"Your friend in there," Victoria says, jerking her thumb towards the restaurant. "I think I could help her out."

"Who, which one?" I blurt out. "Anyway, they aren't my friends."

She looks at me through her glasses. The top halves of the lenses are tinted green, looking kind of like eye shadow. She's got gold press-on letters, V-L-C stuck to the bottom of her right lens. Must be her initials.

"Who are they, then?" she asks.

"Just some people I know."

"They look like friends. What's life without friends?"

It's like my life. What does she mean? But I don't want to argue. I trace my index finger around the title on the movie poster: *Nailed.*

"I'm thinking about Jade, the sharp-eyed one. Zachary told me what she's going through. Rough stuff." I nod and she continues. "I own a building across the street. Down off of Speedway. We could move her and her mom in there. I've got a vacant studio apartment. It's not big, but there's a fresh ocean breeze when you open the windows."

"You don't even know her." I turn around to look at Victoria. The streetlights are reflecting off her glasses.

172

"I feel I do, since she's a friend of yours..."

"No she's not." What is Zachary telling her?

She contemplates this for a moment, then keeps going on. "I'm thinking her mom could work for me in the restaurant. Tell her I'll throw in the rent. Gotta be better then Taco Bell, where she works now."

"Del Taco," I correct her.

She takes a big drag off her cigarette. Then she looks at me funny. Like she's trying to remember something.

"You do look like your dad." She slides close next to me and gives me the biggest hug I think I have ever had in my life. She smells like sweet and sour sauce and smoke. The buttons on her coat dig into my chest, but she won't let me go. I squirm a bit and break away.

She puts the cigarette out on the underside of the bench, but holds onto the butt. "Talk to Jade. Let me know what she thinks. And come back inside, fortune cookies and orange slices all around. Ha." And with that she's gone.

I watch her slip into the restaurant. Through the window I see Zachary and my "friends" talking and laughing at something Zachary just said. They look like they are having fun. I'm not really good at having fun. I mean I can fake fun pretty good, but when it comes down to it, I'm no good at fun.

The Big Blue Bus pulls up. It's the number one and it would take me most of the way home. I turn back to look through the window and there's Zachary looking at me. He stands up and starts to walk towards the front door. I quickly hop on the bus and dig a dollar out of my pocket. I put it into the change box then find a window seat and try not to look back at the restaurant.

It's pretty much a straight shot up Pacific Avenue from Zachary's apartment to my mom's condo. It's weird that I never knew he was so close. I wonder if my mom did. I mean maybe we were at Abbot's Habit sitting next to each other having bagels, or lying in the sand at Muscle Beach one day with our beach towels side by side. It's not like I ever paid attention to men his age anyway. I wonder if he ever paid attention to kids my age? Did he know I was so close? Has he been keeping an eye on me all this time?

I look across the aisle at an old man with shaggy gray hair leaning against the window. What if he's my grandfather? I never even think about my family. Melanee never talks about her family. And she especially never talks about Zachary's. One time in fifth grade we had to make a family tree and I chased Melanee for days, asking her to tell me about my grandparents. She said it gave her migraines to think about them. So I told her I wouldn't go to school anymore since I couldn't turn in my project. She said that was cool and took me to San Francisco for a month. When we got back the school wouldn't let me in since I missed so much. She told the principal to f-off and hired one of the ratty girls to tutor me for the rest of the year.

I get off the bus at the Santa Monica Pier before it turns up Broadway and away from the beach. Then I walk all the way back to my condo from there, along the ragged cliff edge of Palisades Park, high above the ocean, far away from all the pressure. Since it's Friday night the park is full of tourists and the far side of the street is bustling with valets and people going in and out of bars and restaurants.

Lloyd opens the gate for me by hand. It's still not fixed.

"Everything okay, Ms Blu?" What, do I look upset or something?

"Sure, yeah, I'm good." He hits the elevator call button, the door opens and I walk in. I catch my reflection in the glass elevator and don't see why old Lloyd is concerned. I look fine, head held high; no way he could know how I feel. No way. Why is the elevator still going down? Shit, I punched the pool level. I wonder if Zachary thought I looked upset. Jade didn't say anything; doesn't mean she wasn't thinking it. Okay, back up, tenth floor. But then, why would she think it? She hardly knows me. Zachary, of course, *really* doesn't know me. My floor, finally. And now he's stuck with those teenagers and he probably hates me.

I walk into my empty apartment. Why is it my fault everybody's so screwed up? Well, except Penn. He's got it together. And Jade is so confident, most of the time. And Zachary, he seems like he's sort of happy. I guess. Sort of. It's hard to tell. No food in the fridge, of course.

Out on the balcony. Mom says it's a landing on the stairway to heaven. The ocean is shimmering with moonlight. The car lights streak along Pacific Coast Highway. It's pretty awesome that I get to hang out alone and have nobody telling me what to do. Total independence.

Did I run out on Zachary and those other kids? I wonder what's gonna happen to Marley now? How is Jade gonna get home? Is Zachary gonna drive her? Maybe Penn will take her to his house. Oh, man, I shouldn't have left. It's not my fault how I felt. I hardly know any of them. They're not my problem.

I check my cell. I missed a text from Dakota. It says:

NOW? I ignore it. What's wrong with me? Why am I freaking out? I don't have friends. Never did. I mean I get along, but not real friends. It's the one thing my mom taught me: don't trust anyone who says they're your friend. I need to hit something hard.

I go into my room, which I haven't been in, in like forever. I sit down at the drum kit. I pick up my sticks, not my brushes, and let it wail.

Chapter Thirty-five

My cell phone wakes me at ten o'clock in the morning. It's my mom. I find my phone on my dresser and pull it under the covers with me.

"What?"

"I got you a meeting with Bernie the Attorney at noon. They're sending a car for you."

"What? Why?"

"I told you, Kali, I'd get you out of this court thing. Bernie's gonna sort it out but they need you in a meeting."

"It's Saturday."

"They are very accommodating. I told them to make this their top priority."

"But it's all worked out, Mom. I took care of it."

"You did not take care of it, Kali. You've messed the whole thing up and they're punishing you in some police place and no Blu deserves that, even if it is your fault for not working it out with Bernie. You know I'm right. I love you. You know that, right? They're sending a car to the condo at eleven." She pauses dramatically, "You are there, aren't you?

"Yes. But I'm not dealing with your lawyers. I'm handling

this myself."

"Kali, I'm hearing disrespect. Am I hearing you want to go live homeless on the beach? Am I hearing I have to cut you out of my life? You betray me like this after all I've done for you? Is that what I'm hearing?"

Yeah, I'd love to live on the beach and skate forever and never talk to you again, you vicious, controlling monster. Did I say that out loud?

"All right, all right, I'll go to your stupid meeting," I say.

"Wear something outrageous. You're the daughter of a rock star. I want you to represent."

"Okay, okay, okay." I am such a total wimp.

I hang up the phone and look at the clock. I have an hour to get ready. I lie on my back and think about what would be outrageous to wear to my mom's rock and roll law firm? I sit up and see the police hat I left in the middle of the floor. My police school dress uniform. Perfect. She'll be outraged. I wander off to the shower and have a long one.

I find the bag with my uniform stuffed in it. I should iron it, but I don't even think we have one. I put on the blue button down shirt, dark blue pants and tie. I look in my mom's closet for her airplane bag stuff... she's got this enormous bag where she dumps all the first class travel kits and free hotel crap. I dig through it till I find some black shoe polish in a little white plastic container that says *W Hotel - Seattle* on it. I remember that trip. Seattle has an awesome library designed by Rem Koolhaus with big strange spaces you can wander around for hours. I spent all day reading in it while my mom slept off a hangover.

I take the polish and start to shine up her stiletto boots.

They're too big for me, but they look perfect with my outfit.

I try to tie the necktie. Not so easy. Not even sure how. I punch the YouTube App on my cell and type in: HOW TO TIE A TIE. Up pops this cute guy holding a tie all happy to show me how to do it. And what do you know? It works; I'm wearing a tie, knotted firmly, but not too tight.

The building intercom rings. I walk down the hallway like it's a catwalk, hips forward, shoulders back and pick up the phone.

"Yo, what up?" Throwing in a little 'tude.

"Ms. Blu, your driver is here."

"Aight."

I grab my backpack and put on my police hat complete with badge. I check myself out in the hall mirror. Outrageous. I'm out the door.

When I get off the elevator, Lloyd tries not to smile at my uniform as he escorts me to the waiting town car with its license plate that says MUSIC 1. The car smells like lilac air freshener. All these town cars do. They're trying to hide the smell of weed. I open the windows and the sunroof.

We head up Santa Monica Boulevard towards Century City. A couple of skyscrapers loom over the empty roads. Century City is trying so hard to pretend it's a real city. To me it's just lawyers and agents. The car pulls up to the entrance of a high-rise building. The bottom floor is the entrance to CAA, Creative Artists Agency. Otherwise known as the Death Star. CAA is the top talent agency in Hollywood and the agents and lawyers inside make this town run. A valet opens my car door and helps me out. A guard holds the front door open for me. I have to sign in and show my ID. I show them my fake cop badge and the serious security guards don't even think it's weird that a kid is dressed like a cop in shiny stiletto boots. They must see it all here. The lobby area is all shiny white marble, with counters of more shiny white marble, everything way too big and high and beautiful. Like a cathedral, like they want everyone to believe they are something mighty and great. Totally ominous.

I get into an elevator and press floor seventeen. When the door closes the elevator turns pink, and all the walls glow softly. Each elevator in this building is lit with a different color. I used to love riding these when I was a kid.

Bernie's receptionist tells me to wait so I sit down, pick up yesterday's Hollywood Reporter. Penn would love it here. He'd fit right in, dressed sharp, looking busy, holding papers tightly.

"Kal." I turn around and see Chandara, Bernie's assistant. "I thought you were going to handle this by yourself." So snide.

"My mom called this meeting, not me."

She looks me up and down and shakes her head. Her ponytail waggles out from behind her. It's different today: it still goes straight down past her butt but then it curls up right at the end.

She walks quickly down the hallway and I almost have to run to keep up.

"What's wrong, Chandara, aren't you happy to see me?"

"If it weren't for you, Ms. Sunshine, I'd be in Santa Barbara today."

"Four Seasons or San Ysidro Ranch?

"San Ysidro." It's hard not to be fascinated by her ponytail, all shiny black and swaying back and forth.

"This meeting'll be quick, right? You can be up there by dinner time."

"Uhmph." She looks over her shoulder at me. "So who are you wearing today?

"You like it?" I say, spinning around.

"Really, who sewed up those threads?" She's baffled. It wasn't in Vogue. It wasn't even in Marie Claire.

"It's my school uniform. I got sentenced to transfer to this police academy high school magnet."

"No, seriously."

"Seriously, we have to wear police uniforms."

Chandara stops and looks in my eyes, trying to see if I'm screwing with her. I guess she decides I'm not, because she laughs suddenly, loudly.

"Kali the cop! I love it." She gets quiet again. "Your mom's cool with this?"

"Mom? Who cares?"

"Well, Bernie, for one. And me, for two, since Bernie pays me to care."

"She must pay you a lot," I say.

"She doesn't, which is why I don't really care."

"I think your hair got shorter since I saw you."

"Screw you, Kal. Do they give you a gun?"

"No, but I got handcuffs. You into that?"

"Actually, yeah," she says very seriously, like it's a big secret.

"Oh." Not sure what to say. She looks at me like I'm a bug.

"I'm kidding, geez, you're turning into a cop already."

"This place creeps me out."

"It's designed to. A lot of people were paid a lot of money to make you feel uneasy here. What else goes on at cop school?"

"I'm learning to recognize blood at a crime scene. And how to subdue another person with my bare hands."

"Get out of here."

"There's also a law magnet at this school for kids who want to be lawyers."

"Cops, lawyers and teenagers. That could be a TV show." She gets a real serious look on her face and starts to type something in her Blackberry. Everyone in this town's looking for a fresh story angle.

We walk around the corner and she leads me into a weird room, like a conference room, but the big table in the center isn't in the center, it's half built into the wall, with the wall going right down the middle of the table. Chandara sits me down at the table, staring at three huge flat-screen monitors in a row on the wall. The screens are low, almost touching the table where it seems to go into the wall.

"Sit tight, Kal. Bernie will be right with you."

"Isn't she in New York?"

"Yeah," she says as she leaves.

I sit and wait. Suddenly two of the three screens pop and blink. And there's Bernie sitting across from me at the same table in the same room. The screens are like windows that show the other half of the room, with the table looking like it just continues into... New York, I guess.

"Kali," she roars.

"Hi Aunt Bernice." My mom makes me call all her agents, managers, publicists, and lawyers, Aunt or Uncle. 'They're better than family. They actually care about us.'

"What are you wearing, princess? Spin around."

I spin around in my swivel chair. She barely looks.

"Gautier, darling? Must be. So real. It's fabulous." She fiddles around with some papers and adjusts her reading glasses. "We're just waiting for your mother, sweetie, then we'll start."

I didn't know my mom would be on this call. This just gets worse.

"Are you really in New York?" I ask.

"Absolutely. Isn't it just totally magic what they've done with this conference room? Even the carpet matches. And I get to spend precious face time with my favorite troublemaker. Isn't this the best technology?"

"Texting works for me."

Then the third screen blinks and there she is, in all her glory, Melanee Blu. It's kinda weird 'cause I haven't seen her in more than a month. She darkened her hair. I think. Also, she's not in an identical room, so she looks out of place, and it kind of ruins the whole illusion of me and Bernie being in one room.

"Bernnnnnieeee," Melanee squeals in a rusty voice. But she's looking at me. I guess she only gets one camera for both Bernie and me so we can't tell who she's looking at.

"Hello, darling, you look marvelous," coos Bernie. "Who are you wearing?"

"Oh, do you love it? I found a tiny boutique on Maui, actually in Paia. There's this couple who make these. Hand dyed coconut fabric. They use all natural plant dyes. This one is Hibiscus. Isn't it genius? I want to bring them to L.A. Set them up at Fred Segal, but we'll talk about that later." Fred Segal is a small department store with high-end boutiques. As for my mom concentrating long enough to start a retail business... never going to happen.

"Coconut? I want to touch it. Lean over, closer to the camera." My mom actually leans over and Bernie actually pretends to feel her shirt, then they both crack up.

Finally my mom notices I'm sitting here spinning in circles in my Aeron chair.

"Kali, baby. Oh my god , I miss you so much, I just want to cry." She wipes her eyes a bit.

"Go ahead, cry, Mom." BTW, she just wants to cry often. She never does, though. She also never listens to me.

"We're gonna get you out of this mess, baby. You know I'd be there right now, but the Santa Ana's always screw with my nasal passages and you know what that means for a singer and the total dryness makes my hair tense up." She pulls on her straightened hair, grins and winks. At Bernie, I guess.

"*There was a desert wind blowing that night,*" intones Bernie. Oh, no. This.

"*It was one of those hot dry Santa Anas,*" adds Melanee, all breathy and ominous, "*that come down through the mountain passes and curl your hair...*"

"*And make your nerves jump and your skin itch,*" says Bernie, trying to match Melanee's voice but sounding like she swallowed sawdust.

"*Meek little wives feel the edge of the carving knife and study their husbands' necks,*" says Melanee, cool and spooky. Then she suddenly laughs and so does Bernie. Mom loves Raymond Chandler, and I think Bernie genuinely does too.

They've been doing this routine since I can remember.

"That's why we're here today, right Bernie, to get Kali out of this mess?"

"Yes, sweetheart. Piece-o-cake," Bernie assures her.

"Awesomeness. Hey, both of you, my favorite girls, I want you to hear the song I just wrote. Now be honest with me. I'm gonna sing a little bit for you. No judgments. Tell me you love it." I guess she's forgotten about crying and missing me.

Then my mom does what she always does when she's about to sing. She wiggles her hair in front of her face. When she's ready she raises her eyes up slowly, peaking through her brown mass of bangs. She looks right in the camera and sings. She always knows right where the camera is.

I don't want your sorrow
I don't want your pain
I remember what you look like
What you feel like is deep inside
Am I running away to you?
Will you keep me strong?
I feel no love
I feel no pain
I take the scissors and I pull
'til I get the splinter out

She finishes, and Bernie starts applauding, "Perfect. Bravo."

"Kali, what about you, what do you think?" asks Melanee, urgently. "You're not saying anything."

It's actually not a bad song. I guess I should tell her.

"I liked it, Mom."

"No you don't. Anyway, I hate it. Why did I write that piece of crap?"

"Melanee," Bernie interrupts, "It's going to be a hit. Maybe. You never know. I love it. Now let's focus on Kal's situation. We'll get back to your song."

My mom has already drifted off. She's looking around the room, obviously thinking about something else.

"I've put through all the paper-work and spoken to a colleague at Juvenile Court and he's in the process of wiping Kali's record clean and clearing her of her obligation to this Police Magnet they have so inappropriately put her into."

"Can we sue them?" asks Melanee, intensely focused again. "Those monsters forced my baby into their violent police program."

"You can always sue anybody," replies Bernie smoothly. "It's just takes time and money."

"I signed up for that program," I point out.

"But you did it 'cause they gave you no choice," snaps Melanee, suddenly angry. "That's coercion. Do they make you to carry a gun?"

"Don't worry about any guns, Melanee," says Bernie. "As of next week, when the paper work has been processed, Kali will be out of there."

Melanee smiles a big toothy smile. "Aren't you happy, Kal? See what mommy did for you?"

"I guess."

"How's New York, Bernie?" says Melanee. "Anywhere new to eat?"

They start chatting about restaurants and spas and

whatever. So this means what, exactly, for me? I go back to my old school? Have a tutor? Find a new school once again? Do they have a plan for me? I've been thrown out of every private school on the Westside of L.A. Usually because my mom gets in a fight with the administration and yanks me out, or I don't show up for a couple of months 'cause I'm on tour and they kick me out. Or both.

"But before this is official, there is the problem of Kalifornia's custody. Somehow Judge Mitchell awarded temporary custody to Kal's father, Zachary Cooper," says Bernie.

"What?" Melanee screams.

"Sorry to spring this on you," Bernie says.

"You're screwing with me! Tell me you are," my mom pleads.

"This really the first you've heard of this, Melanee?"

"Aaah, yeah! Oh, that will not happen. You will not see your father, Kal. Ever. Bernie, I'm so glad you are stopping this before it starts."

"I'm afraid it has started. Right, Kalifornia? Haven't you been under your father's watchful eye since," she adjusts her glasses and reads a paper, "last Thursday?" She looks up at me over her glasses. I glance over at Melanee, not sure what to say.

"Kali?"

"Mom, you didn't show up at court for me and I could have gone to jail and I had no choice but to find Zachary."

That sets her off.

"Zachary? You found him? What's that mean?"

"Did you know he lives in Venice?"

"You saw him? Are you insane? Do you have any idea what...?"

"He's not so bad, Mom."

"Kali, he's evil. I told you a billion times."

"Well maybe I wanted to see him."

"What?"

"You've kept me away from him for so long," I say totally calmly. "Maybe I wanna know my dad."

"Your 'dad'?" This really pisses her off and she screeches: "Do you call him 'Dad'!?"

She hurls her purse at me... well, the screen, which is really the camera. I actually duck under the table, though I know it can't reach me from 3,000 miles away. She's screaming and ranting, at me mostly, but also at Zachary, and the judge and all of them are pricks and dicks and some other things that are basically the same thing. I just want to stay hidden. Chandara, who must have been watching on another screen in another room, comes running in. She crawls under the table with me. "Come on, let's get you out of here," she says.

We crawl on our hands and knees down the length of the table and out the door. She points me into her office and tells me to stay there as she continues down the hall. I notice she's been researching Police Academy High Schools online on her laptop. Another, bigger, computer shows the videoconference. I see my mom has calmed down and is checking her makeup in a hand mirror. Bernie is busy texting. Chandara comes back with two Cokes in cans. She hands me one while she reads her Blackberry.

"Bernie says she'll sort it out with your mom. I should send you home. She'll call you next week with an update. In the meantime, she wants to know where you've been sleeping at night." She gestures me to sit in her office chair. She takes the guest seat.

I don't know why, but I tell Chandara the whole story, from Teen Court, to taking the bus last night back to my mom's apartment. I don't even like Chandara and I know she's gonna steal all my stories for her screenplay, but at the moment I don't care. Sometimes it's good to talk to someone who listens carefully, who's really interested. Maybe she's being paid to be interested, but it doesn't seem like it. Anyway, I don't think she's used to listening like that either, 'cause when I finish she looks kind of lost and embarrassed.

"You wanna go to the mall or something?" she asks.

"Why?" And I'm thinking what an idiot I am to talk to this idiot.

"I like to go to the mall when shit happens." she says. "Retail therapy."

I shouldn't call her an idiot. She's being sincere. She's even trying to help. We're just from different planets.

"No, I should go," I say.

"I have to tell the driver where to take you. Back to your mom's place? Or your dad's?"

"I don't really want to go either place."

"Well, how about a friend's house then? I have to send you somewhere. I need to show a return receipt."

I think about where to go. I don't have any friends. Dakota is just a hookup once in a while and I'm not into that right now. But I'm pretty curious about what happened with Jade and Penn last night. I don't even have a phone number for

Jade. She might not even own a cell phone. I've never seen her use one.

"Sure," I tell Chandara, "He can drop me off at this girl Jade's house. She lives near downtown."

"She a friend of yours?"

"No. I know her from school."

"I can't just send you anywhere. It's gotta be friend or family."

"Okay, she's my friend," I force myself to say.

Chapter Thirty-six

The town car pulls up in front of Jade's house. I take off my police hat, shirt and tie. Luckily I wore a tank shirt underneath. I throw my shirt, tie and my hat onto the back seat and ask the driver to wait in case she's not home.

I walk up to the front door and knock. After a couple of seconds Jade opens the door.

"What's up? What are you doing here?"

"I thought we could hang. I wanted to hear what happened after I left last night."

Jade peeks out the door at the town car. "Your dad?"

"Just some random driver. Can I stay?"

"I guess."

I turn back and wave for the driver to leave. Jade opens her door wide so I can come in.

The first thing I notice is that the living room is full of beds. The TV is playing and three little kids are sitting on the edge of one bed watching the movie *Ninja's vs. Zombies*. They're still in their pajamas. It's really dark inside the house even though it's a sunny day. A sheet hangs from the ceiling to separate the living room from the kitchen.

Jade pushes the sheet aside and leads me through the kitchen. Cabinet doors are wide open and empty. We step carefully through to another room, a makeshift extension to the house. There's no inside walls, just sheets of cardboard nailed up to the two by fours. A piece of plywood covers most of a broken window.

Weirdly, Jade is relaxed in this environment. She doesn't apologize for the mess. She's acting like it's perfectly normal to live this way. I'm wondering how she can stand it. The darkness alone is so depressing.

She sits on a double bed and picks up a Play Station 2 control and starts to kill bad guys in *Resident Evil: Dead Aim* on the TV screen.

"Is this your room?" I ask."

"I share it with my mom. It's my aunt's house. Those are her grandkids in there."

"You sleep in the same bed with your mom?"

Jade nods yes. I can't imagine anything worse than sharing a bed with Melanee.

"So, how did you get home last night?"

"Zachary had to pick some guy up at the airport and take him to a hotel in Santa Monica. Then he took me home."

"You rode in the limo with the guy in the back?"

"No, I rode up in the front with Zachary."

"Was the guy a creep?"

"Just some businessman, I didn't really look at him. How come you split?"

I shrug, "I don't know. I was just done."

She nods as though she gets it.

The video game makes a sound like she's waited too long

to move. She begins a new game and then hands me another controller. I sit on the bed next to her and we start shooting people together.

Suddenly there's a giant bang, making the walls of the house shake.

"Front door," says Jade.

There's a commotion in the front room. One of the kids starts to cry. A wave of fear rushes over Jade. She suddenly looks like a deflated balloon. "He's here," she says.

"Who?"

"Frankie. Came to pick up his kids."

Now it sounds like all three kids are screaming.

"They don't like him either?"

"If he comes in here, just keep playing the video game. Don't look him in the eye. It's disrespectful." Did she really just say that? I have to respect this man who beats her up and threatens her?

I can hear him on the other side of the wall. He lumbers through the kitchen and into Jade's room.

Now he's standing in front of us and speaks harshly and loudly to Jade in Chinese. I keep my eyes on the game like she said. I can see through the corner of my eye that she's hanging her head down. She answers him back in Chinese with short, clipped sentences. He yells in her face, then, suddenly, whaps her on the back of the head. I spin around, yelling: "Hey, leave her alone."

Jade looks at me, horrified.

I've done it. I've looked him in the eyes.

Jade doesn't say anything but her look tells me to sit down and shut up. I ignore her urgings and try to stare him down.

It's nearly impossible to see his eyes through his dark pupils, but I manage to lock eyes with him. He shouts something at Jade and hits her again and her nose starts to bleed.

"Stop it!" I yell at him, but now Jade is screaming at me to stop. She's really scared. I better back off. Up close like this, Frankie's face is covered in pock-marks and his eyes are steely cold.

Frankie reaches out and grabs my hair. I yank my head away and a dreadlock breaks off in his hand. He looks surprised for a second. Then he starts to laugh and grabs at my hair again. I push him away.

The oldest of the three kids comes in and stands behind him. He holds up my dreadlock for me to take it. I refuse to play his game and that pisses him off even more. He pockets my hair and then yanks the kid's arm and drags the kid out of the room. But not before stopping to turn around and point two fingers at me like he's holding a gun with his forefinger and second finger extended and his thumb raised. Then he turns his hand up upside down, thumb towards the floor, gangster style. "I keep my eyes on you," he threatens in a thick Chinese accent. Then he pulls his finger back and makes a clicking sound with his tongue, like he's just fired his gun.

The front door slams and the kids cry as he drags them out of the house. Jade wipes the blood off her face.

"That's messed up. Are you okay?" I say, picking up a towel from the floor and handing it to her.

"You never should have looked at him. I warned you."

"What do you think he's gonna do?"

"Make my life even heller. You know, I really want to kill him," she says.

"Yeah, I know."

"But I don't want to go to jail. You're right about that." I'm not one to trust anybody and I don't think Jade is either. So far we've got that in common. So I don't know how this is going to go down, but here I go.

"You know that old lady last night? The one who owns the restaurant?"

"The crazy white chick who thinks she's Chinese?"

"Yeah. She's like Zachary's landlord and she told me she has an apartment in Venice you and your mom could move into."

"Like we can afford that?" She laughs at the absurdity of the idea.

"If your mom works at the restaurant, she'll work it out so you wouldn't have to pay any rent. She said."

Jade gets real serious. "You're not shitting me? It's for real?"

"Yeah, she told me last night to talk to you about it."

"Why would she want to help me?" Jade is confused.

"I don't know," I shake my head side to side.

"I don't believe you."

"Honestly. I know it's weird, but it's true." I try my best to reassure her.

"People don't do things like that."

"I think... she said... she thinks you're my friend or something."

Jade eyes me suspiciously. Then she starts laughing. Her laughter is contagious so I start laughing too.

Then I stop laughing and get real serious. "Can you leave now? Like right now?"

"You mean move to Venice now?"

"Yeah. Before he comes back with the kids," I say as seriously as I can.

"What about my mom?"

"You can call her. Tell her the plan. Where is she?"

"At work, in the North end of the Valley. She won't be back till seven."

"We'll pack up everything and then go pick her up. I told the driver I'd call him when I need a ride home." Jade looks at me suspiciously. "Come on, before Frankie comes back."

She hesitates for a second and then jumps off the bed. She picks a lamp up off the side table, which is just an upside-down diaper box. She turns the box right side up and starts shoving things into it.

Then I text the driver: 15 MINUTES. There's another diaper box in the corner. I grab it and start pulling clothes out of a drawer and throwing them in.

Chapter Thirty-seven

Windward Boulevard by the Boardwalk is quiet tonight. The sign strung across the street spelling out V E N I C E swings and bobs in the hot Santa Ana breeze. I love the bare bulbs on the letters and the feeling the sign's been there since forever.

I'm helping Jade and her mom settle into a small efficiency apartment above Tattoo Asylum. Jade's mom is a thin, tall Chinese woman named Lucy. She unpacks the diaper boxes and puts items away. I help Jade put sheets on a pullout sofa bed. Jade's mom doesn't speak much English so Jade has to keep translating between us. Victoria enters the apartment with a tray of tea from her restaurant. As she passes out cups she says something to Lucy in Chinese. Victoria turns to me and whispers, "I just told her she can trust you. Don't let me down."

Lucy speaks to Victoria in Chinese. I watch them talk, not having a clue what they're saying. They seem friendly, even giggling a little.

Jade leans over quietly and tells me, "My mother is very grateful."

Victoria says something else in Chinese then turns to us and explains, "I know some Original Gangsters. They throw protection my way."

"For real, the O.G's will watch our backs?" asks Jade.

"Yes, my dear. They will. While you're here in the neighborhood you'll be safe. You have my word. I've lived in Venice since 1968 and nobody screws with me."

"We'll pay you back," Jade tells her.

"I know, honey."

Lucy turns towards me and says something in Chinese.

Jade translates: "My mother says you have lovely eyes and a lovely grace just like your grandmother."

"Victoria's not my grandmother." What is she thinking?

Lucy protests in Chinese.

"She says you look exactly like her."

"No, I don't."

"You kind of do, Kal," Jade says.

I turn to look at Victoria and she gives me a wink. What?

"I always told Zachary you'd find us," says Victoria, "when the time was right."

"What are you talking about?"

"Zachary's my first born. So that makes me you grandma."

"For real?"

"For really real," Victoria says and she pulls me in tight for one of those suffocating hugs. I struggle away and just stare at her.

"Let's give them some time to settle in." She slips her arm in mine. "Come on over to my place. You can try on my wigs. I bet you'd look real cute as a redhead. I'll pull out my old bunny costumes too. They'll probably fit you. You skinny little runt..."

I look back at Jade as Victoria escorts me out the door. Jade's just laughing, not at me, she's laughing like she's happy.

Chapter Thirty-eight

Victoria has the entire top floor of an old brick building with a wall of windows overlooking the ocean right on Ocean Front Walk. She's showing me around. She stops at a grand piano in the corner of the room. The top of the piano is covered with photos. There's one of a showgirl Victoria picks up and hands to me, a black and white photo in a gold frame.

"That's when I was an exotic dancer. Would you look at those legs?" In the photo a young Victoria wears only sequined pasties and a g-string. She looks gorgeous, with huge feathers fanning from each hand. Victoria sits down at the piano and starts to play an old song as I check out the other pictures. There's one of a teenage Zachary with spiky blonde hair. A baby wearing a red, knit ski cap with a giant pom-pom, is strapped to his back. Zachary sneers at the camera with a 'don't take my picture' look.

"Is this me and my dad?"

"Yep. Pretty cute, aren't you?" My mom got rid of all the photos of my dad. It's weird to see me riding on his back–so dependent on him.

A framed high school diploma sits proudly in the center of

the piano. It has Zachary's name on it but the date is only a couple of years ago.

"Took him a long time to get that." Victoria stops playing and lights a cigarette. "Dropped out of high school when he was about your age."

"It's hard to imagine he was ever my age."

"He really just dropped out, started living on the streets, a real punk kid. Met some street musicians and they got him making music with other people. Before that, he only played alone in his room." She sucks on the white cancer stick and starts pounding out another song.

I sit down on a scratchy overstuffed blue chair by the window. A cat hops up on my lap and snuggles into a ball.

"That's Clementine. Push her off if you want. Big old cat." She is a fat old cat, that's for sure. Looks even older than Victoria.

"There was a house out in Laurel Canyon an old female photographer owned," Victoria says slowly, almost absentmindedly. She's playing some old jazz tune, her cigarette dangling from her mouth, her long fingernails clicking on the keys. "She liked having young musicians around and rented rooms to them. Your mom lived there. And then your dad did too."

"The photographer's name was Florida. My mom talks to her once in awhile," I add.

"She does? Still? I thought she hated Florida."

"Mom says she loves her."

"Melanee had odd ideas about love."

"You mean she wouldn't know love if it bit her in the ass?"

"That's a tad more colorful than I would put it, but yes."

She winks. This lady who is practically a perfect stranger to me is telling me more about my mom and dad than my mom ever told me.

"Zach hooked up with your mom and they took off. Her career took off then too. Your dad didn't want much to do with me. I only ever met you once. The day I took that photo." No wonder she doesn't seem familiar to me.

"How old was I?"

"Not more than a year old. Cute as can be." I blush a little.

"Why did he go back to school?"

"He hit rock bottom several years back. But he sobered up and came back home. First thing he did was get his GED. He's taking some classes right now at Santa Monica College. He tell you that?"

"No."

"Maybe he's embarrassed being a student at his age." The cat has fallen asleep on my lap. I didn't even realize I was petting her.

"Why didn't you tell me who you were before?" I ask.

"That's a fair question." She stubs her cigarette out.

"And?"

"And... how do I know? Maybe I wasn't sure you'd want some sentimental old stripper who smokes too much and talks too much as a grandmother. Maybe I've wanted to see you for so long when it finally happened I didn't know what to say. First time in my life I didn't know what to say. Ha!"

Chapter Thirty-nine

"Why didn't you tell me Victoria was my grandmother?" It's Sunday morning and Zachary agreed to let me stay at my apartment by myself last night only if I promised to meet him and Marley first thing this morning for breakfast. We're on the boardwalk, heading back from the Figtree Café.

"She's bizarre. She wanted to tell you herself."

"Kal, check it out!" Marley jumps up and down because right in front of us is a giant ramp filled with snow. In the middle of October at the beach, which today is like 100 degrees, they've built a snowboard ramp and dumped tons of artificial snow on top from one of those snow blowers. Girls are dressed in snowboard gear with boards and dropping down from the top of the ramp doing jumps. There's a crowd and an announcer. A big green and pink sign overhead says: Supergirl Jam - Surf, Skate, Snow.

I grab a flyer off a table and read. "They've got a half pipe over there and a girl's street skateboarding competition too. You skate, Marley?"

"No. I can't skate."

"You could learn."

"Not allowed to," says Marley. "Absolutely nothing that might scrape or bruise or damage my skin. Roseanne's rules."

"But you don't live with her anymore."

"Hey, now I can. Yippee!" Marley leans back on her heels and wheels towards the half pipe.

"Man that kid, she's a rocket." Zachary runs after her. I'm not running. It's too early in the morning.

I slowly meander towards the bleachers, which are set up next to the half pipe. And look who's leaning on a wall watching one of the skateboard girls warm up. Dakota.

"Hey, Dakota who you watching?" I sneak up on him. He jumps.

"Oh, shit, Kal, a little warning." He's not exactly happy to see me. I'm thinking that's not a good sign. That's when I see who he's watching. It's Hailey. She's one of the Silly Girl's—an all-girl skateboarding team. She's trying to get a jump on every little bump on the half pipe.

"Grab the rabbit," Dakota calls out to her. I throw him a look like, "are you serious?" He looks at me, like, "what do you care?"

Hailey finishes her practice and skates over to us. She has a ring through her nose and wears ear lobe plugs. Her hair is bright orange, in two side ponytails, with a black streak down the middle. She's wearing a Silly Girl tank shirt that lets her show off her tattoos. The Silly Girl logo is a black and white drawing of a Betty—a self confident, stylish, hot chick—with the word "Silly" at the bottom. Hailey's got on short black shorts with red and black striped tights underneath. In Silly Girl style, she looks like a girl, not a boy like most girl skaters.

"Hey, Kal, what's up?"

"Not much. How's it going?"

"My skull hurts and my eyes are dizzy." She lays her head down on the divider wall. "Dakota said you got arrested."

"Yeah." I throw Dakota another look of irritation.

"Did you have to go to jail?"

"No."

"That's cool. I gotta keep practicing so I don't fall on my ass again. I totally ate it twice in the same spot already."

Hailey skates away.

I get right to the point. "Are you hooking up with her?"

He rolls his eyes. "We're friends, Kal. What are you doing here?"

"Yeah? Are you friends with me, too?" I know, stupid, right? But I wasn't ready for this, for Hailey and Dakota, and both of them being friendly to me.

"No, you don't know what it means."

He's right, I guess I don't.

"Zachary's over there. I gotta go hang with him."

"Which one is he?" I point towards Zachary and Marley.

"Can I meet him?" Dakota asks.

"No way. Are you serious?

"Why not?"

"I don't want him meeting anybody."

"Not even your boyfriend?"

"That is so lame, Dakota."

"Why is it lame for your dad to meet your boyfriend?"

"Well, first of all, 'cause I don't really consider him my dad and second 'cause I don't really consider you my boyfriend."

"You're an asshole." He must be really pissed. He never

called me that before. "Why do you keep pushing me out of your life, Kal, like Friday night, I know you weren't babysitting."

"I was."

"You are such a liar."

I'm not sure what to say here. What does he care what I do? He's getting way too close for my comfort level.

"Are you seeing someone else, Kal?"

"Seeing someone? What does that mean? Yes, I see people all the time, so do you, look around." I gesture to the crowd on the boardwalk.

"You don't have to be a jerk-off. It's okay to be close to someone, you should try it once in awhile." He throws his board down and skates away.

Be close to people? He has no idea. Ever since I was a little kid, I'd make a friend and then we'd move away or I'd change schools. I learned pretty early on to keep my distance. It's time to keep moving. I never wanted a boyfriend anyway. I never said that.

I climb the bleachers and sit down next to Marley. Zachary leans across Marley and asks me, "Who was that guy you were talking to?"

"Nobody, I just know him from the skatepark."

"I want to be a Silly Girl," Marley squeals too loudly. People turn around to look at her. Now she's jumping up and down and bringing lots of attention to herself.

"Marley, sit down." She's acting like I imagine an irritating little sister would be except that she's taller and has bigger boobs than me.

"Do you know her, Kal?" Marley asks while she watches

Hailey skate down the half pipe.

"Yeah, sort of."

"She's a rad skater," Zachary says. "I've seen her down here before."

"I like her hair," Marley pipes in. "Maybe I'll do that to mine. Can you dye it for me, Kal?" This kid does not know when to quit.

I see Dakota standing under a palm tree on the grassy mound across from us. I can't tell if he's watching me, or Hailey, but either way it's making me uncomfortable.

"Come on," I say to Marley. "Did you want to learn how to ride a board?"

"Ooooooh, yes!"

The three of us jump off the back of the bleachers and head over to the skate park. The boardwalk is getting crowded. There must be a thousand people out here already. Between the weather and the SuperGirl Jam it feels like a summer day.

"Look, Kal, there's your twin," Zachary says.

"Where?"

"Over there, that girl." Marley points to a white girl with long black dreadlocks. Her clothes are a combo of homeless and hippie and she's got this earth tone patchwork skirt on.

She's swaying to her own kind of music while singing out loud, "I've got a hole in my bowl and no way to plug it."

"I don't look like that."

"Yeah you do." Do I really? Do my dreads make me look like a ratty druggie girl? What a waste of a look. I don't even do drugs.

We follow the ratty girl for a while and she keeps singing, "I've got a hole in my bowl and no way to plug it."

This tall hippie guy wearing shabby clothes that he probably paid a lot of money for flags her down and says, "I can help you out."

She sings, "You can?" She puts on a big smile and skips over to him. I tell myself: I have got to change my look.

Marley starts chatting away about some Rihanna video and I am trying to tune her out when I feel this sharp pain in my arm. I swing around to see what I could have rubbed up against. There's an Asian guy in sunglasses walking backwards in front of me. He pulls his sunglasses down his nose and gives me the most evil look in the world. He takes a final drag on his cigarette and flicks it at me. It's Frankie.

I look down at my upper arm. There's a round burn mark. He burned me with his friggin' cigarette. I look back up, but he's gone, disappeared into the crowd.

"What's wrong?" Zachary asks behind me. I wonder if he saw what happened? I wonder if he knows it was Frankie? And I wonder if Frankie knew it was Zachary in the limo? All I can really think about right now is Jade and her mom. Did we get them far enough away? Are the O.G.'s really gonna keep Frankie from harassing her? I should probably tell Zachary what just happened. That's what you're supposed to do, right? Tell your dad your problems and he'll take care of it? Well, I never had a dad before, so I'm not familiar with the rules.

"I'm okay," I turn back to Zachary. "Just a mosquito bite." I can take care of it myself, just like I always have.

I spin around to Marley and throw my board down next to her. "Slam your front foot forward, lean forward, and whatever happens, don't lean back."

Chapter Forty

Why do people feel heavier when they're asleep? I know he wasn't this heavy when we were awake. I can barely feel my legs with the weight of another body on top of me. I keep watching his calf muscles twitching–like they're having a bad dream. I run my hand over them and my fingers just pulse up and down. And I have another question: Why am I such an idiot? What am I doing half naked under this guy I don't know. I'm so mad at myself I could scream. Seriously, how do I get myself in this kind of situation? Now I have to get him out of here, past Lloyd, who will look away discreetly, which is worse than if he laughed at me.

It happened so quickly, I wasn't thinking. I was starved after Zachary and Marley left the beach so I went to Zelda's Deli. Van, the mini-donut guy was particularly dreamy and he said, "Hey, how ya doing, K?" and I gave him one of my smiles and I was thinking I should move on from Dakota and that's all it took, really, 'cause Van's shift was over and we ended up back here. I guess we fell asleep after messing around a little.

What time is it and why does that hideous noise keep going

on and off? Oh, I recognize that sound now: It's the intercom. It means I have a visitor. A visitor! Not now. Zachary was supposed to meet me here at six. Is it six already? Where's my phone?

I push hard on Van to get him off of me. He falls to the floor with a thunk, clunk, ouch.

"What's happening?" He looks around as confused as I am. Afternoon naps always disorient me.

"You gotta get out of here." I throw him his shirt and reach around to put mine on.

"Why?"

"You just do." The intercom keeps buzzing.

I pick up his shoes and nudge him towards the front door. I push him out to the hallway, hand him his shoes and hit the elevator button. Van is buttoning up his shirt when the elevator opens and who is inside? Zachary.

Zachary looks at Van holding his shoes with his shirt opened. Then he looks at me and I can feel that I have total bed head. And my t-shirt is inside out.

"What the hell, Kal?"

"Zachary, this is Van."

"Get out of here, Van," barks Zachary.

Van backs away, whimpering something about, yes, okay, sure.

"Why are you trippin' on him?" I ask.

"Because you're fifteen."

Van steps inside the elevator. "Call me later, K."

"Grrrrr," I growl at them both. The elevator door closes and Van is gone.

"Are you sleeping with him?"

"No."

"I'm not sure I believe you."

"I'm not sure I really care if you believe me. Didn't you mess around when you were fifteen?" I yell at Zachary.

"That's different," says Zachary.

"Why? Why is that different?"

"Because you're my daughter."

"No I'm not."

I walk into the apartment, past the piano in plastic box, straight out to the balcony.

Zachary follows. "Kal, man, you're just a kid."

"You don't have to get all in my face about that. I know all about the boys and the bees and the STD's." I sit up on the railing.

"Would you get down from there?"

"Why?"

"Because this doesn't feel like a Stairway to Heaven to me."

"What?" How does he know about that? He grins at my recognition.

"I guess she still says that," he says. "Some of us have our eyes on the stars. Your mom does. She was always that way. But I have my eyes on the ground and when I look over this balcony all I see a long fall into the Jacuzzi to Hell."

I shrug. It's too weird sharing so much with this guy. And I stay up on the railing.

"When you were a little baby I'd think about what this moment would feel like when I met your boyfriend for the first time and how I'd want to beat the crap out of him."

"Van's not my boyfriend."

"I don't know if that makes me feel better or worse." He smacks some flying bug between his hands. "How old is he?"

"Seventeen or eighteen, I guess."

"I was seventeen when you were born." That quiets us both. He lies back in a lounge chair. I look out at the sunset over the ocean. The smog from the city has made the sky super orange.

"Where's Marley?"

"Took her back to the group home. Marley likes you, Kal. You're good with her."

"Why don't you just adopt her?" I can't believe I'm asking him this. What does that even mean? It's like asking him for a baby sister or something.

"I can't. I can't professionally and I can't personally." I can see he's frustrated with the question. Well, I don't want to sit here while he gets all emo on me. I jump down from the rail.

"Bathroom." I say and head down the hall to splash some water on my face. I stare at myself in the mirror and study my dreads. I didn't think they made me look ratty, but I've had them for a while and I never like to get stuck with any look that's identifiable. I bet that's why Frankie could find me in that big crowd. There're not many white girls with dreads and now that I saw one, maybe it's time to give up my look.

Zachary's got to be in the big plastic box 'cause I can hear him playing the piano, and it's loud. You're supposed to shut the door, dum dum, to make it sound-proof. I sit down on the toilet and listen. He's playing one of my mom's hits. The one she named after me, *Kalifornia Blues*. It's a sad, slow song, with a heavy R&B rhythm. It's so annoying. I don't know why, but he's got no right coming in here, Melanee's apartment, uninvited and playing her songs on her piano. No right.

"Stop playing mom's song!" I shout out from the bathroom.

He plays more intensely, louder. "*Her* song? *I* wrote this one."

"Don't lie. It was mom's lullaby she always sang to me."

"Pretty sure of yourself, aren't you?" Zachary shouts.

"Why are you lying?"

"Not lying. Check the liner notes. And don't accuse me of lying. Ever. It's one thing I can't stand. Makes you sound like your mom." He keeps playing. I flush the toilet and go into mom's bedroom. I climb up on her bed and pull the framed gold album of *Bullet,* off the wall. I scan the liner notes in the frame and find the song, *Kalifornia Blues*. There is an asterisk next to the name. I run my finger down to the bottom of the notes and see another asterisk. It reads, "All songs on this album were written by Melanee Blu with the exception of *Kalifornia Blues*, written by Zachary Cooper."

I study the image on the cover: It's the picture of a water pistol–the same one he's still got–with water dripping from the barrel. The drips form a puddle and the puddle is in the shape of a heart. Zachary continues to play. I wander back to the Plexi box, my eyes half closed, listening to the music as I drift up to the piano.

"Mom lies about everything," I say to Zachary. "Why didn't I think she lied about you?"

Chapter Forty-one

All I can think about are Jade's icy cold hands as they reach under my shirt and around my back. Her nails are so long and sharp and they give me shivers when they hit my skin. I'm trying not to scream as she threads a wire through the sleeve of my shirt. I'm super ticklish but there's no way I'm letting her find out. Controlling this tickle is torture, but I've learned from experience if I let people know how easy it is to tickle me, I'm a goner. I read somewhere that only children are the most sensitive 'cause they didn't grow up being tickled by their siblings. With a sibling attack you learn to defend yourself as well as train yourself not to laugh. Oh, how I wish I had had a sibling right about now.

Jade lifts up my shirt and tapes a recording device to my stomach–an iPod. Once that's in place, she lowers my shirt. Finally, I can breathe.

"EVIDENCE," Mendoza repeats as he underlines the word on the black board, "ADMISSIBLE IN COURT, SURVEILLANCE. These are all words I want you to become familiar with. Without evidence you have no case against a criminal."

"Enough with the lectures, we've all seen Law & Order," I say to Jade under my breath.

"And even if he or she may be guilty, without evidence he or she can go free." Mendoza looks at me, "Young lady, drop and give me twenty pushups and no chatter during the lecture." Is he kidding me? All eyes on me now while I slide off my chair and onto the floor. Push-up position. Here I go, one, two, I hate cop school, three, four...

"Can someone give me the definition of *admissible*?" Mendoza continues yakking on.

Javier raises his hand.

"Young man?"

"Admissible is something allowed in court," Javier answers.

"Good. Now what kind of evidence is admissible in court? Is what an undercover officer records while wearing a recording device admissible?" asks Mendoza.

Keeba raises her hand.

"Young lady?"

"No," Keeba calls out.

"Why not?"

"Because the criminal didn't know it was a police officer at the time."

"How many of you think Keeba is correct?" About half the class raises their hand. I don't 'cause my hands are busy supporting my entire weight right now, fifteen, sixteen... I hate cop school...

"She's not. If an undercover officer wears a wire whatever he records can be used against the person who says it in court."

"But that just doesn't seem fair to me," says Keeba.

"Why's that?"

"Well, he didn't know who he was talking to. If he was talking to a cop, he probably wouldn't give away anything."

I finish my last damn pushup and sit back down.

"That's exactly why it works. The Supreme Court has said that when a person does not know he is being interrogated by a police officer, even while in custody, it's not considered coercion. The defense is that the criminal chose to offer up the info, therefore, fair game."

"Fair game," I repeat to myself. Then I look quickly at Mendoza to see if he heard me say that. Luckily the bell rings.

"Take the wires off carefully," Mendoza calls out. "Jade will collect them. And don't forget about Wednesday's forensics test."

Now that I am fully wired all I can think about is getting some evidence on Frankie. Have him talk to me and confess to me that he had Jade's brother killed. That would put him away for good.

There are moans from the class as everyone de-wires themselves. Everybody but me. When Jade isn't looking I grab my books and backpack and walk out the door.

As I hurry down the hallway to get to the bathroom before the next bell rings, I bump full on into Penn. He steadies himself by grabbing hold of my shoulders.

"Hey, not so fast, sister. Where you headed?"

"Bathroom. Really gotta pee."

"T-M-I, girl." He's still holding on to my shoulders, then his hands start to crawl around my back. Not something I'd usually mind, but I've still got that damn wire on and...

"You wearing a wire?"

"Uh-huh."

"Am I under investigation?"

"It's not on."

"Okay. So why, then?"

"Cop school, surveillance, bad guys..."

"Man oh man, I've got to keep my eyes on you girls all the time."

"Okay, now can I go?"

"Hold up. You gonna see Jade later?"

"Yeah, she's in my next class."

"Give this to her for me." He hands me an invite to the Beat Boyz playing at the Vera Davis Center in Venice. Eight o'clock tonight.

"Don't I get one?"

"You? No, you've got curfew. Not taking you out after dark again. Learned my lesson, you are trouble."

I'm staring at him, into his eyes. Why am I doing that? I'm not into him, I'm not into him, I'm not into him, I'm not–

"Kal?"

"Yeah?"

"You okay?"

"I really gotta pee." I turn and leave, hoping he can't tell what I'm feeling.

The second bell rings, but I have to remove the wire, so I bolt into the bathroom. I slip into a stall, take my shirt off and lean my butt against the door so that it doesn't open. Some superintendent decided it wasn't safe if we could lock ourselves into the stalls, so none of them have locks. I look down at my stomach with that blue tape all over it and bite my lip. Then I yank the tape off. Yowl, that hurts. I pull the wires out of my sleeves and hide the device deep inside my pocket. Once it's in, I put my shirt back on. I stop at the sink and look at myself in the mirror. I'm not used to wearing my hair pulled back and don't really recognize myself. I touch what's left of the dread that fell off in Frankie's hand. It sticks out a little. I'm wondering what he did with my dread? Does he still have it? Did he toss it? Maybe it *is* time for a change. Now might be the perfect time. But not right now. Now I have to drag my ass to my next class.

Chapter Forty-two

The computer lab is in the nicest room of the school, the one with the hardwood floors and big old windows that open. The room we spend most of the day in is dark and in the subbasement. Shouldn't the computers be in that room where it's dark? Who made these decisions? Probably the same idiot who took the locks off the bathroom doors.

I have to tell the teacher, Ms. Poundstone, why I'm late. "I ate something foul," I explain. She gives me an understanding nod and sends me back to my station next to Jade.

"Where were you?"

"Bathroom."

"Did you turn in your wire?"

"Yes," I whisper.

"There was one missing, I didn't remember getting yours."

"I put it back in the box," I lie.

"Whatever."

I give her the flyer from Penn. I think about not giving it to her, but how lame that would be. She reads it as a little smile crawls across her lips. She notices me watching her and quickly loses the smile.

"What's going on in here?"

Jade points to the front of the room. There's a photo of L.A.'s Mayor Luis della Casa taped to the white dry erase board. He's Latino, about thirty-five, mustache, big old forehead with a receding hairline. His teeth are pearly white and he's got brown eyes. No eyewear or distinguishing marks or tattoos.

"Make a criminal composite shot of him," Jade tells me.

"The mayor?"

Ms. Poundstone tells us we will be honoring the mayor with these shots as he's coming to visit our school next week to give some award to Officer Mendoza for his "excellent program."

I turn on my computer and open up FacePrints. It's the same program that police sketch artists use to render likenesses of criminal suspects. You chose from a series of head shapes, noses, eye color and skin color. You get to move the eyes closer together or farther apart. There's even a pock-mark tool. You can really acne up the perp if you want.

I know I'm supposed to be compositing the Mayor, but my mind keeps wandering. Instead of brownish skin tone, I choose a yellow ocher-ish tone. Instead of round eyes, I choose almond shaped. Instead mustache, I chose clean-shaven. Instead of thick, wavy hair, I choose, buzz cut. And then I go crazy with the pock-mark tool. When I'm satisfied with my composite, when I see his steely eyes looking back at me. I hit print.

Most of the students have taped their composites of the Mayor onto the white board. Jade's standing behind me in line at the printer. I wait for my picture to emerge. As soon as it comes out of the printer, Jade swipes it. She studies it closely and then says, "It's Frankie." I take the picture back from her. "What's going on?"

I lean in real close to Jade and tell her, "Look, I swiped the surveillance equipment, don't say anything but I thought we could get Frankie to confess to killing your brother. That way we can put him away for good and he won't bother you anymore."

Jade looks at me real serious with her head tilted sideways. "Don't. Don't do it. It's a bad idea. He'll kill you."

"Not if we're smart."

"We? Anyway, you're stupid if you think you can get away with that."

"Stupid? He threatened to kill you. And maybe me next."

"I'm telling you as a friend, Kal, drop it."

"I don't trust friends." That does not go over well. It's like I hit her. I'm not trying to be mean, but I guess it did sound cold. Anyway, Jade recovers quickly.

"Then I'm telling you as your partner. Or your enemy, whatever. Don't do it."

She takes her portrait up to the board and pins it next to the others. I hate being called stupid, even if I am acting that way. I sit back at the computer and change my composite to look more like the mayor and less like the gangster I can't stop thinking about.

Chapter Forty-three

It's six-thirty and I'm hanging on the steps outside Zachary's apartment. Did I decide to stay here tonight just to piss off my mom? Or did I just cave in to Zachary's demands that I stay here? I can't help but think maybe Zachary's using me to get back at her. Are we both after revenge? But I don't want revenge, I want... that's the problem, not being sure what I can even hope for from my mom. Why do I ever think she'll change? She won't. She can't. So what does Zachary want from her? Why is he watching old concerts of hers on the TV? What's he get out of it? He's climbing up the stairs now looking tired.

"Been here long?"

I shake my head no and stand up.

"What happened to the key I gave you?"

I shrug. "Must have left it in my other pants."

He lets me in. I toss my bag on the couch and sit down next to it. He takes his jacket and tie off and opens the fridge. He throws me a cold Red Bull.

"You got homework?"

"No."

"Hungry?"

"No."

He drifts around the room and starts talking. "I picked up these two four year-old twins this morning, took them to preschool, then drove their mom around while she had lunch and went shopping, picked up the twins, took them to mommy-and-me-gym-and-swim, then took them all home, but not before stopping at Tito's Tacos where the mom and kids had a secret binge-fest in the back of the car. I've been cleaning guacamole off the back seat for the last hour."

"I don't think I ever went to gym-and-swim." I take a sip of my Red Bull.

"Lucky you." It's going to be a really long night.

I look up at the enormous clock that seems to amplify the time. How many hours am I going to be stuck in here with him? I can tell he doesn't want to be here with me either. I mean not really. I will seriously die with nothing to do.

He starts pacing. It might be the Red Bull kicking in. Oh, god, he's starting to freak out too. "I'm usually up all night, out all night. But we can hang out at home, right? It won't be so bad."

The whole night in here with him?

The clock keeps ticking louder.

This place is so small there isn't any place to even get away. At least at my apartment there's the workout room and the pool and Gleeson's.

Tick. Tick. Tick.

Zachary looks up, "Does the clock sound louder to you?"

I nod yes.

"What would you be doing tonight, if you weren't stuck in

here with me?"

I've got to be careful here. Don't want to give away too much.

"Well, tonight, that lawyer kid, Penn's band is playing at the Vera Davis Center. I'd probably go and see that."

"Come on," he says grabbing his keys. "I gotta get outta here." And he walks out the door, without even waiting for me.

Chapter Forty-four

I feel trapped, like I'll never be able to leave. That's why I prefer the night shift. Sleep all day and out all night," says Zachary.

We're walking really fast down Abbot Kinney Boulevard, stuffing our faces with Abbot's Pizza. I totally agree with Zachary. I'm the same way but I don't want to admit it to him. Don't want him to think we're all that alike.

We turn the corner down California Avenue and walk half a block to the Vera Davis Recreation Center. It's an old building that used to be the Venice Library. Zachary hesitates.

"What's wrong?" I ask.

"I have AA meetings in here."

"Do you not want to go in?"

"No, it's cool. Let's go."

The hall is large, with open wooden ceilings. There's a big fireplace in the back and a band set up in front of it. Right away Zachary sees someone he knows, a big black guy with deep-set eyes. They hug like they haven't seen each other in a long time.

"Kal, this is Artie."

"Hello, Kal, it's a pleasure." Artie engulfs my hand into both of his and shakes while looking closely at me with his warm brown eyes.

"I've known Artie since I was a kid. We both grew up in Venice. Artie was always the big kid." He slaps Artie hard in his fat stomach.

"Look who's on stage," says Artie. We turn our heads to see five teenagers setting up their equipment and one grownup plugging in some amps.

Zachary laughs and then says, "Kal, I'll be right back." I watch him work his way through the crowd high-fiving and power fisting a few people as he goes. Clearly his domain.

"Your dad grew up in the hood. He knows a lot of people."

Yeah, I think, he knows everybody but me. Artie turns to chat up some lady dressed all in pink. I look around for Penn and I see him passing out stickers promoting the Beat Boyz, looking real serious. He's wearing his sharkskin suit and his hot boots. It's just the boots, Kal, I remind myself.

"Hey," I hear in my ear. I spin around and see Jade standing there. "I thought you had curfew."

"Zachary's here."

"Where?"

"Over there." I notice Jade's hair is down and really shiny. She has a super short dress on and platform flip-flops. "Are you wearing make-up?"

"Just lip gloss. Cherry Berry." She smacks her lips at me. She is into him, I knew it. "I'm on the way to the bathroom. Wanna come?"

"No."

She goes off and I make a bee-line to Penn.

When he sees me he shakes his head. "What are you doing here, young lady?" he says in a fake authority voice. "I thought I told you not to come out tonight without a chaperone."

"Got one." I point over to Zachary. "See?"

"Ladies and gentlemen, thanks for coming out tonight to hear the Venice Beat Boyz," Artie announces from a microphone. There is lots of applause and then the Ska band starts to play. There are five teenagers, three white kids and two black kids. Zachary's friend plays the trombone. It's a Calypso-R&B number and I love it. The band plays a couple of songs.

Penn stands behind me and puts his fingers along the back of my neck, then whispers something in my ear. His breath is hot on my neck. This music always gets to me, and for a moment I'm floating. For a moment I forget that it's Jade he's into, not me. I forget until he says her name: "Jade says you want to go after her cousin. Bad idea. Don't be a stupid girl."

"I am not a stupid girl." I turn and get my face right in his face. We are about the same height and I can look directly into his eyes. Our noses are practically touching. "Don't call me that again."

"Then don't be a stupid girl and I won't call you that."

And then out of nowhere I do something really stupid. I kiss him. Right on the lips. Stupid, stupid, stupid. I pull away and turn around before he has time to know what hit him. Before he has time to kiss me back, if he was going to. What did I just do? I can't look at him, not right now. The audience is starting to dance. I spot Zachary at the side of the stage. I'm imagining Jade is still in the bathroom. Good, I'm pretty sure neither one of them saw what just happened. I start moving through the crowd towards Zachary. I'm not looking back at Penn. Not this time.

The trumpet player comes up to the microphone. "For this number, we could use a third guitar. Hey, I see the great Zachary Cooper, all the way from Windward and Pacific, out there. What do you say, Zach, join us?"

Zachary is caught in the headlights of the trumpeter's big smile... then he shakes his head and ducks out the side door.

Should I go follow him? Yes. That way I can avoid both Penn and Jade. I walk out the same side door that Zachary did but I don't see him. I stand under a tree. I'm just far enough away from the building to avoid people, but not too far that I can't see if Zachary walks back in. I get this weird, hard, heavy feeling in my chest, making it hard to breath.

"Hiding?" It's Zachary, loud, right behind me. Jesus, where'd he come from?

"I don't know," I try to explain. "It's just that..."

"Let's get the hell out of here," Zachary interrupts. I nod.

We avoid Abbot Kinney and walk through the residential neighborhood. Most of the houses are little beach shacks that people used as summer homes when the canals were here. Now a bunch of trendy people have renovated the little shacks into million dollar modern homes. We are walking along Market Street, a big wide avenue.

"The wide streets used to be canals full of water," Zachary explains. "You'd paddle a canoe down to your friend's house. And paddle back after midnight. Sweet."

Or just sleep in the canoe, I'm thinking. "Why'd they fill the canals in?"

"Because they were idiots. And the canals were badly built so they kept flooding. And corruption. Lack of imagination. Love of cars. Too many ducks. I don't know."

"I'd much rather be rowing a boat right now. I hate walking places. It's too slow."

"Maybe that's why skateboarding started in Venice. Kids missed gliding down the canals and wanted another way to get around town smoothly."

I wish I was on my board now. But I'm wondering: "Why didn't you want to play guitar back there?"

"Long story."

"We have a long walk."

"No."

We don't talk till we get back to his place. Inside the apartment, I stare at the giant clock on the wall. It reads 8:42.

"Jesus, what are we going to do for the rest of the night?" Zachary looks at me, which means I must have said that out loud.

Zachary walks out of the room into his bedroom. He reappears holding an acoustic guitar. He sits down and starts to play. He plays beautifully, dazzling. I can't believe he didn't want to play with the Ska band tonight. I'm about to ask him about it again, when I see the look on his face, which seems to say: leave me alone.

The streetlight illuminates his scar. I've always been fascinated by scars. I wonder if it's because I remember his so well. How could he get such a perfect clean line across his face? I have my own theories. I bet my mom tried to slice his face 'cause she was jealous he was a better guitar player. Or maybe he got into a knife fight with a gangster in a deal gone bad. Victoria said he lived on the streets; anything could have happened.

"You play guitar?" he asks.

"Not really."

"Good for you. It's a dangerous drug, guitar. Just look at your mom. Just look at me. I learned to play when I was about thirteen. I got arrested, five finger crime. Lifted a bunch of video games from Marshall's. Got six months house arrest."

"Six months at home would for sure kill me."

He changes chords and his fingers dance on the metal strings. "The day before I was supposed to get the ankle bracelet, I dismantled all of my skateboards. I took the pieces down to the boardwalk to sell. You can get a lot more for parts than for the whole skateboard. I made sixty-seven bucks, went to a pawn-shop and bought my first guitar. A Univox Hi-Flyer."

"That's what Kurt Cobain played on stage."

"Yeah."

"Did you already know how to play?"

"Nope. Next day came home with my ankle bracelet and locked myself in my bedroom. Six months later I could play a killer guitar."

"So you're suggesting I learn to play the guitar in the next six months?"

"Would pass the time."

"No thanks." I pick up my backpack and walk down the hall into his bedroom. I know it's kind of mean of me, but it's been a rough night. All this togetherness is stressing me out. At least when I'm alone I can think. I stop in the doorway and look back.

"How'd you learn? They didn't have Youtube back then."

"Listening to records."

I enter the room throw my bag onto his bed. I can hear him playing through the wall. Why does he have so many damn guitars? And they're not just any guitars; this is a serious collection. I strum my fingers over the strings of a Squier-Cyclone electric hanging on the end of the bottom row. He also has a Mosrite up there. That's the guitar the Univox Hi-Flyer was based on.

I take the Mosrite off the wall and sit down on the bed with it. I finger the A, B, and E chords. Why didn't I admit to him I play guitar? What am I hiding? Is it just that I'm creeped out we have so much in common? Is that what I'm afraid of?

I plug the Mosrite into a big Marshall amp, plug that into the wall and start to play the first song I learned, years ago: *Folsom Prison Blues* by Johnny Cash. Perfect for my current prison sentence. When I get to the end of the song, all I hear is silence. Zachary has stopped playing. You don't grow-up backstage at rock-n-roll shows without picking up a few chords.

Then he lays into Folsom Prison. After he gets through the intro he starts singing, his voice a deep baritone, growly and passionate:

I hear the train a comin'
It's rollin' round the bend,
And I ain't seen the sunshine,
Since, I don't know when,
I'm stuck in Folsom Prison,
And time keeps dragging' on,

But that train keeps a rollin',
On down to San Antone.

It's a long cable from the Mosrite to the Marshall, so I stand with my back to the door. I play like the devil, trying to keep up with him.

Chapter Forty-five

I'm running laps around the stadium with the other cadets, sweating like crazy. Something's buzzing… no, vibrating in my pocket and it takes a moment to get it out. Have to keep running; we are so absolutely not allowed cell phones on the track.

"Not now," I say, trying to hide the phone under my hair, making it look like I'm scratching.

"Barcelona. You're coming. The cutest studio ever. I've got a ballad to record. Maybe two. They love me in Spain!"

"I'm on probation, Mom."

"Bernie's on it."

"What about school?"

"You're adorable. Limo will pick you up Wednesday morning."

"Tomorrow?"

"Told you I'd get you out of that mess, Kali."

"Maybe I don't want to go with you." That stops her for a second. I speed up my running; gotta stay in the middle of the pack so Mendoza can't see me talking.

"Don't give me that shit, Kal. Your own hotel room. Any

gratitude for that?"

"I don't want my own hotel room!" I yell back at her just as Keeba closes in on me. I think she heard me say that 'cause she's giving me such a look right now.

"How about if you don't come I can't record. I need you. I'm insecure. You're my rock. Don't screw with me, Kal. We're in this together." Anybody listening in might think my mom was desperately in need of my help, but they haven't heard her go on like this my whole life.

Mendoza glares suddenly as we jog toward him.

"You're on your cell? Cooper, are you completely insane?" I have a feeling Keeba ratted me out 'cause now she's looking at me with this kind of fox-like smile–salivating.

My mom keeps blabbing on, so I tell her, "Then you can tell my teacher why I'm gonna miss my forensics test tomorrow." I toss Mendoza my phone as I jog past. He catches it easily.

"It's my mom. You talk to her," I yell at him. I keep jogging. I'm surrounded by kids who want to be cops and I'm nothing like them. I'm the daughter of a rock star. Tomorrow, I could travel first class half way around the world. I have nothing in common with these kids, nothing at all. I bet I can run faster than any of them, if I try. I'll show them. I push ahead, bursting out in front. Free of the jostling I accelerate away. But only for a few seconds. What am I doing? And why? I ease off and let the pack catch up and envelop me. It's kind of intense here, in the thick of it, bumping elbows, sweating, kicking Keeba in the calf sort of accidentally, her looking back like she expected it, not angry. I've never been in a pack before, never had any friends, or even enemies; never got this close to people. It's not like anything I've felt. It's weird. I can't tell if I like it or can't stand it. I'll have time to decide: we have to run for the next half hour.

Chapter Forty-six

We're in the locker room changing into our dress uniforms. I still don't have shiny boots, so I already know I'll be marked down for wearing my Vans at inspection. But what do I care? Apparently I'll be in Barcelona tomorrow. I'm not sure what I should do now. Am I excused from school? Should I go home and pack? I'm just waiting I guess, till someone tells me the plan. Mendoza held onto my cell phone so I can't talk to my mom now even if I wanted to. I imagine there's an email in my mailbox with a flight itinerary.

But the truth is my moms' plans change constantly. The one thing about my mom that I can count on is that she can't be counted on. She might decide at the last minute to record in Rome, or Japan. If I get all excited or prepared, then I'll be waiting at the airport in Barcelona while she's at the train station in Tokyo. I've learned not to take her plans too seriously.

Jade's changing next to me. We haven't talked all day. I'm pretty sure Penn wouldn't have said anything about the kiss, but still, I just can't look at her right now. And I really don't want to see Penn again. So maybe going to Barcelona is the best thing. It'll be like entering my own witness protection program.

Jade's gonna start to wonder why I'm not talking, so I better come up with a good excuse. Before she can ask me I turn to her and say, "I think I'm getting a sore throat." I change my voice so it sounds all garbled. She nods, then tosses me a Hall's throat lozenge from out of her locker. I pop it in my mouth and pretend to be grateful for the nasty menthol tasting thing. She's not telling me anything about Penn. She's not even acting like she has something to tell me. Maybe nothing happened between them last night.

Jade pulls a brown paper grocery bag from the top shelf of her locker and hands it to me.

I open the bag and pull out a pair of very worn in black combat boots.

"They're my brother's. I think they'll fit you," she says.

"Why?" I look at her curiously.

"I didn't want you getting written up again. Mendoza'll make you stay after school to clean out the toilets or something else that really sucks."

"Thanks," I say in my fake horsey voice. I toss my Vans in my locker and slip my feet into the boots. He must have had small feet, 'cause they almost fit. I lace them up carefully and then walk around.

"He was wearing them when he died."

A weird jolt flies through my body. Okay, this is getting creepy. But what do I do, take off the boots and give them back? It's like she really wanted me to have them. Maybe it's part of her culture, maybe I should feel honored to be wearing his boots.

The bell rings and Jade runs out with the rest of the cadets. I don't have time to change my shoes now. I walk out of the locker room wearing a dead guy's boots thinking they'll protect me from getting written up and cleaning out toilets, but not so sure they'll protect me from Frankie. Is it the smartest idea to be wearing the boots of one of his victims?

Chapter Forty-seven

I think about Jade's brother all day. This quote Ms. Poundstone read to us from *To Kill a Mockingbird* keeps going through my head, *"You never really understand a person until you consider things from his point of view. Until you climb into his skin and walk around."* Because all our classes are threaded together with a police theme, Ms. Poundstone explained that detectives often try to metaphorically walk in the shoes of criminals to get inside the criminal mind. Victims too. Retracing a victim's last steps can sometimes lead to their killer.

After half a day in a dead guy's boots, I don't think I can get any closer to inside his skin. While I'm walking, I think about where he took his last steps. When I hear music playing in the quad, I wonder what song he last listened to. What kind of music was he even into? Was he the one that introduced Jade to Pepper? I have no idea.

"You wanna eat at Dogtown Dogs with Penn and me? Jade asks, interrupting my most recent morbid thought–*what was her brother's last meal?*

I'm so not ready to face Penn after last night. So I say, "No,

I'm going to the cafeteria to get some soup. For my throat."

"Right on," Jade says and wanders off down the hall with Penn who avoids looking at me.

I open the cafeteria door and face the boring food. There's nothing here I want to eat. If I were to pick my last meal, I'd have to say it would be Tots with Cheese from Dogtown Dogs with Penn sitting next to me. But that's not happening and right now I'm focusing on Jade's brother. What did he eat? I won't go for the obvious, the meatloaf or the salads or yogurt. I pause in front of the refrigerator case and stare through the glass door. The red grapes with whipped cream in a white Styrofoam bowl catch my eye. Disgustingly perfect for a last meal. After paying, I find a vacant table in the corner. I sit on top of it, not on the bench. My legs are criss-crossed.

I finger the laces of the boots. I wonder where he bought the boots. Or how he paid for them. Maybe he stole them. Maybe they were hand-me downs. Maybe they were his dad's. I realize I don't know anything about Jade's dad. She never talks about him.

We learned in forensics class to look at the bottoms of the victim's shoes for clues. I turn the sole of the left foot over to study it. The rubber heels are worn down so you can see the leather part of the heel. That means he dragged his feet when he walked. The sole is worn down too. He had these boots for a while. I turn over the right boot. It's worn down in the same places. There's some writing on the bottom, scratched in with a ball-point pen. I run my finger over the letters. He must have been left-handed 'cause of the way the letters are slanted. I can barely make out what it says. I lift my foot up close to my eyes and squint. It says: FRANKIE then a series of numbers, probably a phone number.

I feel goose bumps on my arms and put my foot back down on the table. I lean back against the wall and suck the whipped cream off a grape. He must have called Frankie, gone to meet him and then Frankie killed him.

"Cooper, feet off the table, now." Mendoza? Where'd he come from? I get down from the table and jump to attention–legs together, right hand at my forehead, eyes focused forward. This is what we're supposed to do when the officers address us. It's the most humiliating thing, 'cause all the other kids in the room are laughing at me. At least it feels like they are.

"At ease," he tells me. I relax my stance. But I don't look at him. I'm sick of his bullying. What's he going to do, kick me out? I'm going to god damn Barcelona tomorrow anyway. Here's my chance to tell him what I think.

"Sir, before you start on me, Sir, I don't want to be in your precious program any more than you want me in it. I hate this uniform. And I'd rather go to Juvenile Hall than do one more push-up. Sir."

"I'm sure that's all true," he says slowly, nodding. "But you're wrong about one thing." He pauses, looking at my tray. "What is this crap you're eating?" He helps himself to a grape draped in whipped cream and makes a mess of his fingers getting it into his mouth. He licks his fingers clean, looking at me. He gets even more serious.

"I want you in my program." *What?* But before I can speak, he goes on in his quiet, careful way. "On the beat, the heart of policing is being able to count on your partner. Now, don't get me wrong, I'm proud of my teaching; I can teach you almost anything cop related." He pauses, watching me like forever before continuing: "But I can't teach trust. You know what I'm saying?"

"No, I don't," I say, honestly. Then, the weirdest thing, he holds out his hand. Like to shake hands. So I do.

"Jade told me what you did for her," he says.

What did I do?

"And for her mom."

It was all Victoria's idea. I didn't do anything.

"After lunch, go by and see Judge Mitchell. She needs to talk to you."

"The judge? Why?"

"I'm not at liberty to discuss it. You remember what room she's in?"

"What...?"

He interrupts by handing me my cell phone.

"Your mom hung up before I caught it. Too bad, I would have enjoyed speaking with her. But next time, stow the damn thing in your locker." He takes another of my whipped cream covered grapes, more deftly this time, and moves on.

Chapter Forty-eight

Y ou are officially off the hook. You no longer are
obligated to partake in the Police Academy Magnet. You
no longer have any obligation with Teen Court and you no
longer have a police record. Wiped clean." I'm standing in
front of Judge Mitchell's desk, not believing what I'm hearing.

"What happened?"

"Your lawyers were not as understanding of my
unconventional punishment as Penn was. They pointed out,
correctly, that I had no right to do that. They pointed out also
that they would initiate proceedings to have me disbarred if I
did not reverse the sentence immediately. And sue me in civil
court. And go to the school board. And slash my tires and give
me a wedgie. Well, practically." She holds out some papers to
me and continues: "I didn't realize just how badly you wanted
to get out of the program. You should have come to me and
told me."

I stand there, no idea what to say. Not sure what to think,
even. I take the papers and look at them. "I am under orders to
apologize to you, which I can do sincerely, since I actually
thought you were okay. I checked with Penn just a few days

ago and he assured me you were doing well. As did Officer Mendoza. Your lawyers claim Mendoza and Penn are lying. Somebody's lying, but it's out of my hands now. Please let me know which school you will be attending and I'll have the office forward your transcripts there."

"So that's it?"

"As of right now. I've informed Officer Mendoza. You can clean out your locker and turn in your uniform at the end of the day."

"He knew about this?"

"Yes. We spoke this morning."

"I just saw him and he didn't say anything about it."

"It's my job to tell you. Not his. And one more thing. You no longer are required to live with your father. Your mother now has sole custody of you." I just stare at the judge, really confused. "Is there anything else?" she asks.

"No."

"Well, good luck, Kalifornia. I wish you well. I was hoping a little discipline and hard work would do you good, but I guess your mother thought otherwise." I start to leave when I remember the pen Zach lifted from her desk on the first day. I dig it out of my backpack and put it back on her desk. She picks it up.

"Damn, now I owe Julio ten bucks," she says with a little smile. She was betting against me. And Mendoza was betting on me.

Well, this is what I've been asking for, to get out of the damn program. I hate being a cop. I hate this uniform and the curfew. At least now I won't have to see Penn again–ever again. How can I face him now anyway? He makes me way too nervous.

Or Jade either. Or Zachary. I can walk away from the whole thing like it never happened. I can go back to life like it was. Skating with Dakota when I'm in town, traveling around the world with my mom. Total independence. Why wait till the end of the day? Why explain it to anyone? Why not start right now?

I walk out of the judge's office and down the hallway and don't look back. I don't go to my locker. I don't go to turn in my uniform. I just keep walking. The security guard stops me at the front door and I show him my letter of dismissal, so he lets me go.

I get outside and my phone rings. It's Chandara. I stop under a palm tree and answer.

"What?"

"I've been trying to call you all day. How're you doing?"

"Okay."

"Bernie got you out of the cop school and your sentence. That must feel good."

"Yeah." Not really.

"We're sending a car for you at five o'clock tomorrow morning. Bernie wants you with your mom in Barcelona. Your flight leaves at 8:27 A.M."

"Does Zachary know?"

"He only had temporary custody. We are advising you not to talk to him anymore. Bernie wants you back with your mom right away, then she'll sort it out with Zachary. Probably send him a big check to leave you alone."

"I don't know, Chandara. What if I don't want to go?"

"Why wouldn't you?"

"It's complicated."

"You have to, Kal. Barcelona, missy, the land of sunshine and palm trees. Like Hawaii, but with art."

"I thought L.A. was the land of sunshine and palm trees." I run my hand across the graffiti covering the palm tree right next to me.

"I'll be in the car when it picks you up. Since you'll be an Unaccompanied Minor, I have to escort you to the gate and sign for you myself."

"What if I don't show up?"

"Don't mess with me, Kal. I'm skipping my morning power yoga class to take you. Five o'clock at your apartment, tomorrow morning. Hasta la vista, missy."

She hangs up and I feel so mad right now, so used. My mom doesn't care about me or want me in Spain. Her lawyer does. Shit, I hate my life.

I'm looking at the Dogtown Dogs truck parked out front and thinking about those Tots with Cheese. The last customer has picked up his dog and is walking away from the truck. He's got short-cropped hair, shiny white sneakers, and a pock-marked face: It's Frankie.

I stay behind the tree thinking he can't see me from here. He gets into the driver's side of a big minivan parked in the school zone. Just the sight of him heats me up. I know how Jade feels now. I want to kill him too. I hate the way he looks, his chains and shiny new shoes. I hate the way he walks like he owns the friggin' world. I'm worried that he's gonna keep going after Jade and now that I'm leaving, I'm worried he'll go after Zachary.

He must be waiting till school's over to harass Jade. I

should warn her. I look back towards the building and realize there's no way I want to go back in there and face any of those people again. No way I want to explain to them that my mom's billion-dollar law firm has just released me from my sentence and this school. No way.

So for whatever reason I have in my crazy head, I start walking over to the minivan. Maybe it's Jade's brother's boots that have given me the courage. Then I remember the surveillance equipment. Since I don't have the time to wire myself up, I slip it out of my pocket just enough to find and hit the record button. No idea if it will record anything down in my jeans, but what the hell.

Then I lean in Frankie's window and give him a big smile, as fake and as big as I've ever done.

"What the hell you doing?" Frankie says with a mouth full of dog. He seems genuinely confused, so I get right to the point.

"I want you to leave Jade and her mom alone."

He laughs, spitting his Morning Commute–bacon wrapped dog, topped with a fried egg–across his vinyl seats. He's easy to amuse. But I'm serious, so I repeat myself:

"I mean it. Leave them alone."

He's busy brushing Morning Commute off his seat. Then he turns to me with a sneer I think he thinks is a smile.

"Maybe you work for me instead of Jade."

"Yeah, you think? Am I a fair trade?"

"Yeah, you cute, I like your hair." He laughs, reaching for it. I lean back so he can't.

"What do you want me to do for you?"

"Make my clients happy. They like white girl."

"You'll pay me for that?"

"If you are good." He leans over and tries to kiss me. His disgusting face is about an inch away from mine. I quickly turn away. He turns on the anger just as fast. "You shy girl?"

"No, I'm not shy." I turn back and challenge him. But I'm an idiot. I'm trying to get him to say something incriminating, but he's just playing with me, like a cat with a mouse. And my recorder is down in my pants, anyway, useless. I'm starting to feel really vulnerable right now, wondering why I would do something like this. I wonder if Jade's brother leaned on Frankie's car unannounced the night he was killed. Was he demanding from Frankie the same thing I am–that he leave Jade alone? I turn to go when he speaks, sounding calm and reasonable.

"How come I should listen to you?"

It's a good question, really. Why should he listen to me? I need to think about it from his point of view, climb into his skin. Why does he want to hurt Jade? I have to think about the psychology of the criminal. If I learn more about him, I can get him to talk to me. But he answers his own question.

"I don't listen to you," he says, matter-of-factly. "You listen to..."

"Leave her alone," I interrupt. I guess he hates being interrupted as much as he hates being looked at in the eye, and I'm doing both. That must be why he opens the glove box and takes out a hunting knife.

"It's sharp. You understand?"

"You're going to knife me? Is that what you're saying? Right here?" He disgusts me, and the knife fills me with a kind of anger I can't even explain. I can't believe he's pulling a knife on me in front of my school. I lose it. I spit in his face–which goes red with anger in a flash. He wipes my spit off furiously.

He opens his door suddenly, leaning his weight into it, slamming it into me, knocking me down... I stumble but recover, and run. It takes him a moment to get out, just enough time for me to get a few yards head start. But he's fast, and gaining. I dodge around a couple of cars, the change of direction giving me a momentary advantage. He's not as quick on the turns, but that's not going to help me much if he's going to throw the knife at me. I can't really believe he's going to attack me, not here, in public, on campus.

I am so angry at myself. So incredibly pissed off. He probably has a gun hidden under that hoodie. This worthless pig is going to kill me and probably then Jade and I've screwed it all up, my whole life, totally, for nothing.

But Frankie, leaning over a dirty Dodge Ram truck, is suddenly looking weird. His mouth hangs open further and his eyes go wide. He stops swaying and freezes, his eyes darting about, not looking at me anymore. He's looking past me. What's wrong with him?

I turn around. Keeba runs towards my right. I turn left and there's Stefan. I spin all the way and watch the rest of my class running towards us, all in their police uniforms. They fall in line behind Keeba and Stefan just like we do during drills. Jade slips between me and Keeba. She doesn't look at me; she's keeping her eyes on Frankie. She's looking him in the eye, her head high, with a hint of triumph in her own eyes now.

Frankie's still standing there. Probably too proud to back

down.

Stefan steps close to Frankie. "Get the hell out of here." He sounds menacing and strong, not the wimp I thought he was. Keeba steps right up next to him and then Javier joins them.

"Kal, do you have your phone?" Keeba asks. I pull my cell out of my pocket. Keeba takes it. "Get off the campus or I'll call the cops," she says fiercely.

Then like a choreographed dance number, my classmates take one step closer. Frankie bends his head sideways and looks around at all of us. I'm not sure if Frankie's scared or confused, but whatever his thoughts are at this odd moment he backs away towards his van but not before hurling a wad of spit in our direction.

The cadets stand at attention until Frankie is securely inside his vehicle and driving away.

"At ease," Stefan calls to the group. The cadets relax and start high-fiving each other. "Cooper," he says to me, "you good?"

"Yeah, I'm good."

"We heard you weren't coming back. We came out to say goodbye. That's when we noticed you could use some backup," he explains.

"That true, Kal? You're not coming back?" asks Jade.

The bell rings and Stefan melts back into a geek. "Can't be late for Trig." The other kids start running towards the building. Some of them fist pump me and say goodbye as they leave. Jade stays back.

"What were you doing with Frankie? You gotta be careful, Kal."

"What about you? You looked at him in the eyes. You

disrespected him."

"I guess I suddenly felt safe for a friggin' second." The second bell rings. "Guess you're not going to Trig?" Jade asks.

How can I explain to her that I'm being shipped first class to Spain in the morning?

I shake my head, no.

"Kal?"

"Yeah?"

"We got your back, you know."

Jade, not waiting for a reply, runs off and disappears into the school.

I've never felt so distant, so useless, so left out. I can't stand it. There's a bus pulling up and I run to catch it. Without looking back.

Chapter Forty-nine

A big moving van is parked on the roof of my building. Some movers are carrying furniture and boxes. It looks like Gleeson's stuff. I ask Lloyd what's going on.

"Ms. Gleeson and the baby are gone. Her husband got a big movie, they're moving to New Zealand. Two years is what she told me."

I don't believe it. I jump in the elevator and hit number ten. I get off on our floor and her door is open. It's pretty empty inside except for a big glass coffee table and a couple of boxes.

"She didn't even tell me." I say out loud. My voice echoes in the emptiness.

I look around the apartment; it's like she was never there. I open the walk-in closet and reach for the cord light that hangs from the center of the room and pull it. It's empty. I walk through the apartment looking for clues, anything that might explain why she left so quickly. I look out into the hallway between our two apartments.

There's a box sitting outside of my apartment door with a drawing from Stella. It says: FOR KALI. Inside the box are

Gleeson's Doc Martins.

I slide down against my door and start crying like a friggin' baby. I don't know why. I just wanted her to be here. I wanted to talk to her. Why didn't she tell me she was leaving? I throw the boots into the side of her door. One of the moving men comes out to see what the noise is. I pick up the boots and storm into my apartment.

I used to imagine that Gleeson was my mom. That's why I'd watch Stella so much. I'd pretend Stella was my sister and Gleeson was my mom and even though we never saw our dad, it was okay 'cause we did everything together. Gleeson never drank or drugged. She's been clean and sober since she got pregnant. Her addictions now are innocent; self-help gurus and shopping. I can't believe she left without telling me.

I pull off Jade's brother's boots and line them up next to Gleeson's. I study how similar they are to each other. Both black Doc Martins, both worn as everyday boots, both abandoned by their owners and given to me. I lie down on my stomach so that I'm eye to eye with the boots. The owners are gone but their boots are still standing. Am I supposed to wear them and carry out their dreams, continue their lives somehow? I study the boots hoping they'll give me some answers.

I put Gleeson's boots on and lace them up. They're more comfortable than Jade's brothers'. I wander around the apartment scowling and trying to imagine what it was like to be a punk rocker in Washington Square Park harassing tourists in 1979.

I don't even have Gleeson's email address. I can't even thank her.

Maybe she has a Facebook page.

I power up my computer and open Facebook. I type in Gleeson's name. Nothing. I don't think I'm ever going to see her again. And if I go to Spain tomorrow, I probably won't ever see Zachary again. Not if Melanee and Bernie can help it.

Maybe Zachary's on Facebook. I type: ZACHARY COOPER in the Facebook search box. Kinda hard to believe, but there he is. I click on his name, which takes me to his page. I'm allowed to open his photos–just a bunch of random stuff, things from his weird art collection.

Oh, man, how am I going to tell him I'm going back with Melanee? Maybe he'll be relieved; he only had temporary custody after all. And like Chandara said, he'll probably get some big payoff check. I'm sure he can use it. He knew eventually I'd be going back to live with Melanee.

Live with Melanee. That's an oxymoron because I'll never see her. I'll have my own hotel room. She'll sleep all day and record all night. And then she'll make me hang out in the recording studio with her. She'll go on about how she always has sucky recordings when I'm not there, like I'm some god damn lucky rabbit's foot.

But I know I can't stay in LA if she's not here anymore. My mom hates Zachary. She'll do anything she can to keep me from seeing him. And her lawyers are super strong. I don't have any choice. Why am I even thinking about staying? It's not like I want to live with him. There's not even any room in his apartment for me. I knew this was going to all end someday. It's not like they'd let me live by myself forever. Somebody was bound to notice.

I send Zachary a friend request. He must be online 'cause

he friends me right back. I keep looking through his photos when my instant message box opens. Zachary wants to chat.

Zachary: What RU doing?

Kal: Nothing.

Zachary: See my pics?

Kal: Yes.

Zachary: Got any plans tonight?

Kal: I'm going to Spain with Melanee.

Zachary: Seriously.

Kal: I am serious.

Zachary: WTF?

Kal: She needs me.

Zachary: Define 'needs'.

Kal: She's recording. I'm her lucky rabbit's foot.

Zachary: U wanna go?

Kal: Duh... it's Spain.

Zachary: And your sentence, school... what about that?

Kal: Not to worry. The Big Guns got me out of all that. I'm free now. And so are you. They're gonna send you a check to leave me alone.

Zachary: I'm coming right over.

Kal: No. I'm at the airport. About to board.

Zachary: When will I see you again?

Kal: We can text and FB and shit.

Zachary: That's it? After seven years we're just gonna be Facebook friends?

Kal: I guess. I gotta go.

I get offline fast. I don't know what else to say. I mean write. I mean chat.

My cell phone pings. Penn sent me a text: JADE SAID YOU'RE NOT COMING BACK TO SCHOOL. WHAT'S UP WITH THAT?

My head is spinning and I don't know how to explain to Penn what my life is really like. How would he understand? I turn my phone off quickly. No more communicating–too dangerous.

I'm going tomorrow to Barcelona, a fresh start, a second chance. Or would this be my third chance?

I open the closet door to get my suitcase and catch the reflection of myself in the hall mirror. My wrinkled police uniform, my dreadlocks looking a mess, like a lion's mane. I remember that girl on the boardwalk who had the same hair and Frankie taking one of my dreads. I remember how Penn told me I had no business posing as a Rasta and realize I never read that book he gave me. I dig inside the closet and look for the big pink toolbox somebody gave my mom as a gift once. I know there's a pair of scissors in there.

I find the pink handled scissors and stand in front of the full-length mirror. Slowly I reach for the longest dread and I snip it off, right at the top of my scalp. Then I take another and cut it off. It's amazingly simple to cut them off. How quickly my dreads fall to the ground. I feel like a mermaid swimming in a pool of golden hair.

When the last dread is gone I run my fingers through what's left of my hair and trim a couple of random pieces. With my earrings showing and my dirty blonde hair spiking up, I look like Zachary did in the picture on Victoria's piano. I wonder if that's what my mom will think when she sees me in Spain tomorrow.

Chapter Fifty

It's five o'clock in the morning and I'm wearing the pair of jeans Dakota drew on, an old Pretender's t-shirt Gleeson gave me, and Gleeson's combat boots. My new hair is kind of radical shocking, but I'm getting used to it. I lift my shirt up and pinch for fat. The intercom buzzes. Lloyd tells me the Town Car is here.

I drag my luggage into the hallway and double bolt the door. Then I enter the elevator for the last time until who knows when.

There it is up on the roof waiting for me, all black and shiny and looking like it's one of those evil cars in the movies that as soon as you get in a bomb explodes and everyone dies. And there's Chandara leaning on the trunk, texting. She drifts away, distracted as Lloyd opens the trunk and puts my bags in carefully.

"Have a lovely trip, Ms. Blu."

"Thanks." I toss him a little smile.

The driver opens the back door for me and reaches down to take my skateboard. I shake my head and pull it into the car with me. Chandara slips in from the other side.

"Cute hair." She reaches over to run her hand through my hair and then it's back to texting.

My head feels so light without the weight of my dreads. I lean against the window. I don't feel like talking so I'm glad Chandara's busy with her cellphone.

The driver takes the car out of the parking garage and down Ocean Avenue past the pier. The Ferris wheel lights are on but it's not moving. The sun is starting to rise.

Chandara puts her cellphone away. "What are you thinking about?" she asks.

We're still on Ocean, past Fraser, where I crane my head to see if I can see Dakota's house.

"Boys."

She looks out the window too.

"No you're not. Not with that look."

Ocean turns into Pacific and we drive past Dudley. There's the house where we rescued Marley.

"Lawyers, then."

"Bullshit," says Chandara.

We pass Ping's Place, and Zachary's apartment and I can see his wall of guitars through the open window.

"Why'd you cut your hair?"

"I don't know. Time for a change."

We drive by Windward Circle, where Jade lives with her mom now.

I feel kind of sick to my stomach as the driver makes his way through the Marina, past the endless boats, then up Lincoln Boulevard by the Ballona wetlands towards LAX, towards the airport. Lincoln takes a long curving left up the bluffs to Westchester.

"This hill looks like it'd be fun to ride on a skateboard," says Chandara.

What does she know about good hills? Still, it's true.

The driver stops at the red light at the top of the hill. The pedestrian crossing light counts down from Fifteen. Fourteen... Thirteen...

"Spain will be a good change from all this."

"Give me a break." Jeez.

Twelve... Eleven...

"I'm guessing going with your mom isn't the change you're looking for?"

For the first time since I've known her, Chandara sounds like she's from my planet. What's going on with her? Nine... She's reaching out her hand to touch me... Eight... Seven... No way I'm letting her touch me: I turn away, scrunched up, like a coward, scared of everything. Especially scared she'll see my eyes watering.

Five...

Chandara finds my hand and holds it for a second before I yank it back. "You'll be eighteen soon and can do whatever you want. But right now your mom needs you."

I look up at the traffic light, those flashing red numbers telling me not to do something again and again. Chandara looks up at the light... and at me. She gets it, she knows what I have to do.

"Kal, don't do it."

Two... One... and I jump out, throw my board down and skate the sidewalk, down the hill. Smooth. New pavement. Nice. I look behind me. Chandara and the driver are climbing out of the Town Car, watching me. The cars lined up behind them are starting to honk impatiently.

The Santa Monica Mountains stretch across the horizon to the north, the sky still dark, but with just the beginning of light in the eastern sky. At the bottom of the hill, to the west, the Ballona wetlands lay down flat for a couple of miles to the shore. It's protected land, meaning you can't go in, but I'm going to risk it. I hop the wood railing, slip into the tall rushes and try to avoid falling into the lake. It's kinda magical, so not L.A., even if it's all totally designed and built by humans to try to look like it did before humans ruined it. Birds really like it here and they flutter and scramble and flap away as I come strolling through. Have to keep to the left, close to the bluffs, to stay out of sight. Over along the road there's a path for tourists to look at the wetlands. There are a couple of early morning bikers on the bike path. I'm not the wildlife they came to see.

Half way to the ocean the new wetlands end and the ground is boring dry grass, but still pretty wild and empty. The sky's getting lighter. I walk over to the road and skate the last half-mile into Playa del Rey. It's a little beach community. Dakota told me once about this boarded up old motel out here with an empty swimming pool. I figure now is the perfect time to find it. It's pretty early in the morning, so not many people are out. I cut down a side street and walk for a couple of blocks. There's the Del Rey Motel. It is so wrecked and there are 'No Trespassing' signs all over, but what have I got to lose? What are they going to do? Arrest me? Send me back to the Police Magnet? Start the whole thing all over again? Anyway, the pool is around to the side so you can't see it from the road. I figure this is a pretty good place to hide out for a while till I figure out what the hell to do next.

I climb through the chain link fence, step through the high grass squeezing up through cracks in the concrete and sit on the edge of the pool. I try and imagine what it looked like with water in it and people sunbathing. It looks pretty crappy now. I check out some of the graffiti on the inside of the pool. I recognize Dakota's tag: a big circle with the letter L through the middle. The end of the L forms an arrow. I wonder if Dakota will bring Hailey here now that I'm gone?

I pull out my cell. I missed one text from Chandara: BERNIE PISSED. YOU GOT 24 HOURS TIL NEXT FLIGHT. CALL ME LATER, MISSY.

Okay, that's good. I've got a day to think, a day to myself without having to be an Unaccompanied Minor, one more day of freedom, maybe my last day of freedom. Maybe I'll just stay here until the cops come. I'll resist arrest and they'll send me to Juvie Hall. Maybe I can spend the rest of my teenage years in one of those lock-downs in the desert where you have to do manual labor in the hot sun. Maybe I'll pretend to be a loony and get sent to the psycho ward. Or maybe they'll just send me to one of those country club drug rehabs for celebrity kids up in Malibu. I hear you get your own room with a view of the ocean and a private chef to make vegan or veggie meals if you want. They've got poetry classes and horseback riding. Too bad I'm not a druggie.

Maybe I can get Bernie to send me to one of those French boarding schools where you wear uniforms and drink wine at lunch. I could go to Cirque du Soleil school up in Montreal. See, there are hundreds of options besides going to Barcelona with my mom.

My cell phone pings with a new text. It's from Zachary: HOPE YOU HAD A GOOD FLIGHT. LOVE U. He loves me. Since when? He never said the L word before. He believed me when I said I flew to Spain last night. I guess he's up early. Probably having coffee at Intelligentsia. A double cappuccino with a heart shaped swirl in the foam. Maybe it's the heart that put the word 'love' in his mind. I imagine he's sitting alone on that hard backed bench in the front. I never did go to Zuma Jay with him. He's right. I probably could use some new trucks. I wonder if the kids in Barcelona even skateboard?

I text him back: MISSED MY FLIGHT. AM HANGING OUT AT THE OLD DEL REY MOTEL. Soon as I hit send I freak. What am I doing? I just sent it, the message, without even thinking. He doesn't want to deal with this, with me. He was counting on this custody thing being temporary–just till Melanee got back–he said. Can I un-send the message? I search the message App on my phone looking for the delete key. Too late, he just texted me back: BE RIGHT THERE.

What's my problem? It's okay, he can always say 'no'. No to what? I didn't ask for anything. I just gave him my location. I have to stop thinking. I pocket my phone and place my board on the lip of the pool and stand on it, tipping it, looking around, wondering why I like it here so much, why I love the boarded up broken windows and the bougainvillea crashing all over everything and the graffiti like fungus smothering the pool. I can smell the seagull and pelican poop drifting over from the breakwater. For some reason I'm pretty sure it doesn't get any better than this. I drop into the pool. Smooth. The air is cold down in the deep end, cooling me down. My mind is clear. My heart is like ice. And I am totally in control.

Chapter Fifty-one

My cell phone rings. It's Zachary.

"Hello?"

"Trespassing again?"

I stop at the edge of the pool and look around. I spot him squeezing through a hole in the fence. He looks so angry; what was I thinking texting him where I was? Of course he's mad at me, now he has to deal with me and custody and I better say something before he yells.

"You didn't need to come."

Not sure he heard. He's still trying to get through the fence: he's stuck, with his shirt caught in the broken wires. Finally he gets himself untangled and pulls up his sleeve-which shows a big scrape. And I see he's not angry, he's just in pain. We both pocket our phones.

He comes over to the pool and sits down on the edge, his feet dangling and kicking like a kid. He doesn't say anything for a long time and I certainly don't have anything to say, so we're silent, looking around the ruined pool, the weeds all around the lip. They're kinda pretty in the early morning sun, the sunlight just edging down from the lip onto red and orange graffiti of a twisted something exploding. Zachary stares into the dark shadow of the deep end of the pool.

I realize he's watching the very bottom where flowering weeds are growing in a puddle of dirt. It's like a miniature landscape, a tiny island almost lost in all this concrete and spray paint.

"How long you been here?"

"I don't know. Since sunrise."

I drop into the pool, skating the whole bowl in big swoops, grinding the lip, cutting tight curves around the island of weeds. Zachary watches me; he seems sort of mesmerized. I'm pushing myself hard as I can. Then it hits me: I'm showing off, I'm trying to impress Zachary, make him think I'm... I have to stop this thinking. He's not my father, not really. The minute I think he is I'm setting myself up for the biggest crash, disappointment, betrayal ever. I have to stop this; I know better.

"Why don't you play in a band anymore?" I ask.

"I stopped that a long time ago."

"Why?"

"I used to only perform drunk. Stage-fright. So when I quit the booze I quit playing."

I stop on the lid. "That's ridiculous. You gave up?"

Zachary snaps: "I didn't give up. I won."

I push off the lip and drop, but the rear wheels catch and I slide off the nose straight down, my legs running in air, barely keeping up as I reach the bottom and run it out.

"You're a great skater, Kal."

"Thanks." Not what I expected. I run up to the shallow end and jump up onto the lip.

Zachary picks up my board from where it's still hanging at the edge of the pool. "It's been a long time," he says and stands up, comes over to the shallow end of the pool, positions my board on the lip…

"What are you doing?" I yell, "This isn't like cruising…"

But he's already dropping in, a quick circle around the shallow end then down to the deep part and back up, smooth and tight.

"I grew up in Venice, did some time in empty swimming pools," he says, stopping next to me, catching the nose of the board. "Ran into Jade last night. Victoria's got both her and her mom working in the restaurant," he says. "She told me you and the rest of the class kicked Frankie off the campus."

"Yeah, I guess."

"He can't bother you anymore."

"There's more where he came from."

He sits down next to me. "What's going on? Why are you here when you should be in a five-star hotel in Barcelona?"

"I don't know."

Police sirens wail in the distance. We both freeze like we're guilty of something. Well, we actually are. We're trespassing.

"You can stay with me, you know. I'm not afraid of Melanee." I look into his blue eyes. The little creases around them are deep 'cause he's smiling. Like he wants me to stay with him, not like some judge is forcing him into it.

"You aren't afraid of her Big Guns?"

"Yeah, sure I am. So what?"

The police sirens are getting closer. Someone may have seen us and called the cops.

"But I'm not taking the fall for you. Let's get out of here. Now."

I grab the skateboard from Zachary and drop in, around the deep end, back up to the shallow end, hold the rim and flip my legs high over my head–motionless for a moment–then fast across the courtyard and through the torn fence. I turn back and see Zachary running after me, a twinkle in his eye like I've never seen before.

ABOUT THE AUTHOR

Kendell Shaffer grew up n Baltimore, the daughter of two ballet dancers. She moved to the Big Apple for college where she attended Tisch School of the Arts film school at New York University. After college, she moved on to Los Angeles where she produces and writes for television.

Now a resident of Venice Beach, Kendell teaches screenwriting to teens at high schools throughout Los Angeles for the Writer's Guild Foundation.

In addition to spending time with her family, she co-founded Garage Band Venice, a musical jam where kids learn to play music together in individual bands. She raises bees on her rooftop and plays the drums in her living room. Please visit Kendell at http://www.kendellshaffer.com.